SONGBIRD

OF THE

WEST

Center Point
Large Print

**This Large Print Book carries the
Seal of Approval of N.A.V.H.**

SONGBIRD
OF THE
WEST

JAMES CLAY

CENTER POINT LARGE PRINT
THORNDIKE, MAINE

This Center Point Large Print edition
is published in the year 2018 by arrangement
with the author.

The text of this Large Print edition is unabridged.
In other aspects, this book may vary
from the original edition.
Printed in the United States of America
on permanent paper.
Set in 16-point Times New Roman type.

ISBN: 978-1-68324-928-3

Library of Congress Cataloging-in-Publication Data

Names: Clay, James, author.
Title: Songbird of the west / James Clay.
Description: Center Point Large Print edition. | Thorndike, Maine :
    Center Point Large Print, 2018.
Identifiers: LCCN 2018021287 | ISBN 9781683249283
    (hardcover : alk. paper)
Subjects: LCSH: Large type books. | GSAFD: Western stories.
Classification: LCC PS3603.L387 S66 2018 | DDC 813/.6—dc23
LC record available at https://lccn.loc.gov/2018021287

SONGBIRD

OF THE

WEST

Chapter One

S keet Jones placed both quivering hands in his pockets as he walked toward the brothel. He didn't want Amos to notice his fear.

"Bob's Place!" Amos declared in a loud, approving voice. "Good name, nice and simple like. The place I use ta go to, back near Dallas, was called Pretty Patty's Palace. Too fancy, don't yuh think?"

"Reckon." Skeet's voice was almost a squeak. They were now getting close to the two storey wooden structure.

"What wuz the name of the last whorehouse yuh visited?" Amos inquired.

"Can't recall."

"Well, I've been comin' by Bob's Place fer goin' on five years, ever since I signed on at the Bar T. You're gonna like the Bar T, kid, and you're gonna like Bob's Place even better!"

"Reckon." Skeet's heart began to beat faster as they neared the four stairs leading to the wide porch which fronted Bob's Place. Skeet Jones had worked at the Bar T for two weeks and Amos had been good at "showin' yuh how's we do things."

But Skeet didn't want Amos to know that at the

age of twenty-one he had never known a woman, least ways, not in a biblical sense. His fellow ranch hands where he used to work had somehow figured that out and rawhided him mercilessly, which is why he left the job and the area where he had been employed.

Amos continued to gush about Bob's Place as they walked up the steps. "Calhoun may be a small town but let me tell yuh, Bob runs a first rate house. The gals are jus' great. And tonight Bob's promised somthin' really special."

As they walked into the establishment, Skeet wanted to turn and run. Women were sitting around in . . . well . . . their underwear, or maybe it was their bedclothes. It was all sort of the same thing, he reckoned.

Nobody paid any heed to the two newcomers and that was fine with Skeet. Trying to keep his eyes off the women, he noted that the room was large, with red carpeting. A long, plump sofa ran along the far side wall of the room. Two smaller sofas formed a V in the middle of the room, and four chairs sat along the wall beside the door where he and Amos had walked in. A staircase fronted the entrance. A small piano stood tucked away in the corner between the stairway and the opulent sofa.

There were a few lights flickering on the wall, but only a few. Skeet figured they kept it that way on purpose.

Skeet also noticed something unusual about the room, or maybe it wasn't so unusual. There seemed to be a division between the rich and the regular fellows. Jones recognized the tall, muscular man with iron gray hair sitting on the far sofa.

"That's Mr. Jack Sather, the owner of the Bar T," he whispered to Amos. "Almost didn't recognize him. He's dressed in his Sunday best . . . ah . . . on a Saturday night."

"Shush," Amos quickly replied. "We don't speak to Mr. Sather when we're here. Jus' pretend yuh don't see him."

"Sounds crazy—"

"Shush!"

Despite the fact that there were many men standing around in the room, Jack Sather had the sofa to himself. There was no woman sitting with him but that seemed to be his choice. Sather looked very content as he slowly sipped the amber drink in his hand.

Skeet followed Amos, who walked to the back of the room where several men were standing around trying to look busy as they did nothing at all. "Got more jaspers here tonight than usual," Amos continued to speak in a whisper. "It's the somethin' special I wuz tellin' yuh 'bout. They say she's one fine filly!"

Jones surveyed the other "fillies" in the room. There were four in all. Two of them were occupying the middle sofas, laughing at the jokes the cowboys sitting beside them were telling. Even standing a few feet behind the sofas, Skeet could tell the laughter was forced.

The other two women were perched on chair arms with one of their own arms around a man occupying the chair. One of them had bruises on her face which powder couldn't completely hide. The other was so thin as to be skeletal. Her eyes had a glassy, faraway look.

Skeet Jones's mood began to change. Instead of feeling scared he was starting to feel angry, though he didn't know who he was angry with.

A shadow moved quickly down the stairway. At the last stair it stopped and lit a kerosene light which was fastened to the wall. Only then was it apparent that the shadow was a woman. To Skeet's relief, the woman was fully clothed; the most distinctive aspect of her appearance was long hair that reached almost to her waist. After completing the task with the light, she hastened to the piano and sat down.

The stairway was now fully lit and a well-dressed man charged down it, stopping half way and waving at those assembled like a politician at a fourth of July picnic. He was greeted with shouts from the men: "Where is she?" "Whatcha got for us Bob?" "Time to keep your promise, Bob!"

"That there is Bob Hoover, the owner of the place," Amos whispered to Jones.

Skeet nodded his head. "I sorta figured that."

Hoover now had both hands raised. If not for the wicked grin creasing his black bearded face, he'd have looked like he was being robbed. "I won't keep you waiting long, gentlemen. Tonight, I'm gonna present a new gift to our fair town. A gift so new, she hasn't been unwrapped yet, if you get what I mean!"

Raucous laughter filled the room. Skeet's anger became laced with disgust. Part of that disgust was aimed inward. How could he have allowed himself to be shamed by men who spent their time at places like this?"

Bob continued. "Our new arrival is sent from heaven. A real angel." He pointed one hand up the stairway. "She's coming down from the clouds right now. Angela the Angel!"

A young blond girl, dressed in a low cut white gown, began to walk down the stairs to loud, appreciative catcalls and whistles. Skeet reckoned Bob's statement about the girl coming down from heaven wasn't all that much of an exaggeration; only heaven could have produced such a beautiful creature. Her face was perfectly proportioned and her eyes a breathtaking blue.

But Skeet Jones noticed something else about Angela's face. At first she had been smiling but as the girl looked around the room, those blue eyes reflected terror.

In a display of mock gallantry, Bob took Angela's hand and walked her down the remaining stairs and to the piano. The rest of the men in the room didn't seem to notice the girl's obvious fear or maybe they didn't care. They continued their loud shouts.

Bob's voice roared over the clamour. "I said I had something special for you gents, well I ain't no liar!"

Boisterous cheers thundered over the room. Angela's face was now pale and her smile fragile.

Hoover draped an arm over the girl's shoulder. "Today is a very special one for our angel. Tell us about it Angela."

The girl looked uneasy, as if afraid she would be mocked. "Today is my thirteenth birthday."

Bob's smile became broader. "Only thirteen! Gents, our angel is going to get more beautiful with every passing day!"

Loud whoops filled the room. Skeet wanted to yank his six gun from its holster, fire it in the air and tell all the jaspers to be quiet. For a moment, his eyes fused with those of Angela. The girl seemed to be looking at him pleadingly; maybe it was because he was the only man in the place who wasn't yelling and acting like a fool.

"I promised to give our angel a very special

present," Hoover had laughed before he spoke. Skeet noted that it was a strange laugh: four short guffaws in a row, sounding a bit like someone impatiently knocking on a door.

The owner of the establishment continued. "Angela likes to sing, and I told her she could sing here tonight. After you hear her, I'm sure all of you gents will want to come back to Bob's Place very often and enjoy Angela's beautiful . . . voice."

There was more ugly laughter from the crowd but it soon subsided as the piano started up and Angela began to sing. Skeet knew little about music but he could recognize a magnificent voice when he heard it. The beauty of the girl's singing was made more poignant by the harsh room she was performing in.

The song was *Aura Lea*. Skeet had always thought the song mushy. But then, he had never heard it sung by Angela the Angel.

> Aura Lea, Aura Lea
> Maid with golden hair;
> Sunshine came along with thee,
> And swallows in the air.

Jones could tell he wasn't the only man affected by the girl's voice. The expression on the faces of the men went from lustful to dreamy. When Angela was finished the applause was loud

13

and respectful. Several men began to call out for another song.

The owner of Bob's Place noticed that the mood in the room had changed and he didn't like it. Hoover began to shout over the demands for Angela to sing again. "Gents, we're now moving into another part of our angel's birthday celebration. Angela, I want you to meet our town's leading citizen, Mr. Jack Sather."

Sather arose from the sofa and walked over to the girl. "Good ta meet yuh, Angela. Happy Birthday."

"Thank you, Mr. Sather. It's nice to meet you."

"Call me Jack."

"That don't seem right, sir. I mean, you're old enough to be my grandpa."

Suppressed laughter bounced across the room. Many of the men had their faces down and a hand over their mouths. No one wanted to be seen laughing at Jack Sather.

A nervous twitch bolted through Bob Hoover's body. He needed to regain control of the situation. "Ah, Angela, Jack Sather is the man I told you about. The man who would, ah, spend some time with you tonight."

"Well . . . yes . . . but I don't understand. . . ."

"I'll help you unnerstand, just fine, honey," Sather grabbed Angela by the arm. "Now, you come upstairs with me."

Sather's tight grip frightened the girl. "Please,

let me go!" Her eyes became moist as she looked to her boss. "Mr. Hoover, can I sing another song? I don't want to—"

The ranch owner dropped all pretense of cordiality. "Listen, honey, I paid Hoover lottsa money, and it weren't to hear no singing. Now you—"

"Let go of her, Mr. Sather." Skeet Jones did a few quick steps to the front of the room, creating a curious foursome: Jack Sather, Angela, Bob Hoover and now, standing beside Hoover, a cowboy with a hand poised over his six gun.

Sather laughed contemptuously. "Max, this here jasper looks kinda familiar. You recognize him?"

Max got up from one of the sofas in the middle of the room and faced Skeet. Max was the ramrod at the Bar T. He ruled by fear and brutality. Amos had warned Jones about the ramrod. Cowhands who defied Max often ended up leaving the job with broken arms or legs, and a few had just disappeared.

The ramrod's face gushed with an obscene eagerness, like a coyote getting ready to grab a rabbit in its mouth. Max now had a chance to humiliate a man in front of an audience that included women, a treat he could never enjoy at the Bar T.

"Yep, Mr. Sather, this here jasper calls hisself Skeet Jones. I hired him a few weeks back."

Tobacco stained saliva shot from Max's pudgy face. "Looks like I made me a big mistake."

Jack Sather kept his grip on Angela whose face was pale. Bob Hoover remained on the other side of Angela, his smile now trembling. Skeet took two long steps away from the threesome, which placed him in a direct line with Max.

The ramrod spoke in a low, threatening voice as the people on the sofa scattered. "You're finished at the Bar T, Jones. Leave town. Now."

"I'll leave, and I'm taking the girl with me." Skeet replied.

Bob Hoover's bellow conveyed rage. "You're loco! Angela works for me. I already paid for her dress. She's agreed—"

Jones cut him off. "Angela has agreed to stuff she don't understand. No girl should get pawed by some codger just because the old coot can afford to hire a fat saddle bum to do his dirty work."

Skeet Jones was not a gunfighter. His eyes had shifted to Bob Hoover when he spoke to him. But Jones still saw Max go for his gun. Skeet was not a fast draw but neither was Max. Skeet got off the first shot which burrowed into Max's ample stomach. The ramrod staggered backwards, collapsed and began to scream as he rocked about on the floor, "Somebody git me a doc, fast!"

Yells crisscrossed the room. Skeet began to

16

chortle. Max was a typical bully. All those stories about him breaking arms and legs were probably nothing but—

"Look out!"

The warning came from Angela. Skeet turned to see Jack Sather pull a gun from a shoulder holster under his coat. Jones fired as the ranch owner began to aim the Smith and Wesson in his direction. Sather's head seemed to explode as a violent spasm yanked his body upwards then dropped it to the floor.

The sight of Jack Sather being shot threw the room into a hushed quiet. For a moment, there was only the sound of people drawing in their breath.

"My God!" Bob Hoover crouched over Sather's body.

"He's dead!" Hoover shouted. "I can't believe it. Jack Sather's dead!"

People began to run toward the corpse, some shouting curses, others just shouting. Amos was suddenly standing beside Skeet. "Git outta here, boy. Right now!"

"But, it was self-defense. Sather drew on me, I had—"

Amos replied in a fast intense whisper. "That don't make no never mind. Jack Sather owns this town, or he use ta. They'll kill you. Run while yuh still can."

Amos pushed Skeet toward the front door.

Jones took another look in the direction of the fallen ranch owner. His eyes once again met those of Angela. She was standing beside the piano, her entire body trembling.

Skeet ran to her and grabbed her by the arm as Jack Sather had done. The cowboy hoped Angela understood his motives. "Come with me, we're getting out of here."

The couple had taken a few steps toward the door when Bob Hoover suddenly appeared in front of them. "Where the hell do you think you're going? That girl is my property, I—"

"Get out of our way!" Jones shouted.

"The girl stays here, I own—"

Skeet slammed a fist into Hoover's mouth. There was too much noise in the place to hear the squishing sound from Hoover's lips and only a few people even noticed when he fell to the ground.

"Soombody ge' she'iff!" Hoover yelled as Skeet and Angela ran out the door.

"Where's your horse?" Skeet asked as they stood on the front porch of the house.

"I haven't got a horse . . . sorry!"

Jones let go of the girl's arm and took her hand. "Follow me."

They ran toward the town's one general store where Skeet had his large chestnut tethered. He helped the girl onto the horse. "We'll have to ride double for a while. I just got paid. We'll stop at one of the small ranches 'round here and buy you a horse."

"Won't they come after us?" The girl asked as Skeet settled in behind her on the chestnut.

"Not for a while, I reckon. Them folks at Bob's Place were plenty confused. Let's hope they stay that way."

As Skeet spurred his chestnut into a fast run he felt fear and confusion. He had just wounded one man and killed another one. But, as Angela's body pressed against his, he realized he had done the only thing he could. Exhilaration coursed through him and he realized his life could never be the same again.

Chapter Two

Seven Years Later

Rance Dehner woke from a restless sleep and stared into darkness. At first, he didn't recall where he was. He was lying in a strange bed in yet another hotel room somewhere in . . . Texas. Yes, he was in Dry River, Texas. The detective had arrived in town a few hours before and talked some with the sheriff. Then he had checked into the room, taken off his boots and dropped into bed with his clothes still on.

Clumsy steps sounded in the hallway. "A rich man, I . . . gonna be king of the world!"

Dehner sighed deeply. This always seemed to happen. On nights when he got to sleep in a hotel bed, his slumber was disturbed by some drunken fool.

For a moment, an odd sense of depression came over the detective. Was his whole life going to be spent moving from one hotel bed to the next? Of course, he spent more nights sleeping under the stars than in a hotel.

The detective laughed softly to himself, alleviating the depression. How the poets loved to rhapsodize over sleeping under the stars! Rance figured those poets didn't spend many nights actually sleeping outside.

"Gonna have anything I want, 'cause I'm the best there is!"

Dehner tensed up. The voice was shrill with threat. Of course, it could be just drunken bravado, but . . .

A door somewhere down the hall opened. Heavy footsteps clomped into a room. The voice remained loutish though a bit muffled. "None better . . . lots of money . . ."

A loud shot resounded through the second floor of the hotel. In almost one movement, Dehner was off the bed and into his boots, strapping on his gunbelt which had been hanging on the bedpost.

The detective opened the door of his hotel room cautiously. At the far end of the hall, a blade of kerosene light cut across the floor. A loud, moronic laugh came from the other side of the partially open door.

Dehner moved toward the slash of yellow. Two doors in front of him a head protruded from a dark room.

"What's goin' on?" The question came from a bony face topped by long, greasy black hair.

"Don't know," the detective replied. "Get back in your room."

"I'm a farmer," the man spoke as if that fact

lent him moral superiority. "Only come into town now and again. Towns is evil places."

"Get back in your room." The head withdrew into darkness, like a small creature retreating into a shell.

The laughter suddenly stopped. Laughing man had heard Dehner talking. As Rance drew closer to the lighted room, the door was pulled open wider, creating a small swath of light which also splattered a murky tinge of yellow against the opposite wall.

The detective could hear anxious, erratic breathing coming from inside the room. Someone was waiting for him.

Rance Dehner stepped into the light and faced the man who had disrupted his sleep. He was young, maybe twenty, and stood at a fraction under six feet. His hair was sandy and his arms were muscular, ending in large hands. In one of those hands he held a Colt .44. The gun was pointed at the floor.

"Howdy!" He shouted at Rance.

"Hello."

"My name is Holt Conley. Ever heard of me?"

"No. Can't say I have."

"Well, you're gonna! Say, you with the hotel?"

"No."

"If you were, I was gonna tell you not to worry none 'bout that bullet in the wall." He pointed with the .44 toward a side wall. The gesture

23

was casual. He was using the gun as if it were a school teacher's pointer.

"See, I was practicing my draw. Gotta kill a man tomorrow. Know how much I'm gonna get paid?"

"No."

"Two hunert dollars! I ain't foolin'." Conley holstered his gun and pulled out a billfold from a side pocket of his buckskin jacket. He yanked out a fistful of bills and waved them at his companion. "One hunert dollars! Get the rest of it after the job's done. Won't have any problems payin' to get that wall fixed."

As he observed Holt Conley, the detective realized his earlier assumptions had been just partially right. The young man's eyes and words spoke not only of alcohol, but also of madness.

Returning the money to his billfold, Conley stuffed it back into his pocket. "When I checked into this hotel, I told 'em to give me the finest room they had. The clerk said he'd give me the room with the biggest window." He pointed behind himself with his thumb. "Bet you ain't got a window that big in your room."

"You're right!" Dehner noted that the window was unusually large for a hotel. The curtains were red, thick, and clean, another unusual find.

Holt Conley was obviously delighted by Rance's concession. His eyes took on a friendly, though condescending look. "I didn't catch your name, friend."

"Guess I didn't toss it to you. The name is Rance Dehner."

The friendliness left Conley's face, replaced by an intense fire. "Well, now, we got ourselves an interesting situation here, Rance Dehner."

"What do you mean?"

"You're the man I've been paid to kill."

Chapter Three

Conley's right hand became a blur as it propelled downward. His .44 had cleared leather when Dehner's first shot cut into Holt Conley's chest. The gunfighter folded into a jackknife position and staggered backwards.

"Drop the gun, Holt, now!"

Conley raised his right arm and tried to aim at his adversary. Rance's second shot ripped into the gunman's shoulder. He dropped his .44 and again stumbled backwards, this time crashing into the window. The sound of breaking glass mixed with Holt's loud scream of pain.

The detective ran to the window. Holt Conley was hanging outside, his right arm wrapped around the curtain, which he had pulled out the window. Conley was desperately trying to lift his wounded left arm but couldn't manage it.

Rance tried to reach down and grab Holt but the curtain ripped and Conley fell. Another loud scream filled the air as Holt Conley hit the boardwalk.

Dehner ran out of the room and down the stairs. When he arrived at the boardwalk, several people were watching from across the street and a few more were gawking through a large window from inside the hotel. No one offered any help.

The detective crouched over the fallen gunman. Blood zig-zagged from Conley's mouth and then streamed down his neck. His eyes were open, but the wide eyed expression on his face was ghastly, as if he were watching death descend upon him.

Dehner didn't bother with comforting words about getting a doctor. "Holt, who hired you to kill me?"

". . . I only saw her in pictures . . . you know . . . the kind that come in the cigar boxes . . . was gonna see her in person . . . spend my money on her . . . so beautiful . . ."

"The name, Holt, I need the name of the man who wants me dead."

Conley lifted a fragment of the red curtain which was still in his hand. "Is this from the room?"

"Yes."

"The best . . ." He giggled for a moment, then all of the amusement departed from his face and there was nothing there at all.

Dehner looked around. Groups of people were now scattered about watching him. No one came near.

That odd sense of depression returned. He felt very alone.

Chapter Four

Rance Dehner mused that he had spent a lot of time in sheriff's offices, but this particular visit was more than a little different. Outside, a band was playing a tune that, the detective supposed, was intended to be rousing and upbeat. The band seemed to be heavy on horns and drums and light on practicing. Their rehearsal sounded a bit like a dirge for someone that no one was very sorry to see dead.

Sheriff Tal Streeter stood behind his desk instructing a group of four volunteer deputies on the finer points of crowd control. The lawman could brag about having the neatest, most well-dressed deputies in the west. And the happiest. If smiling was a key component of law enforcement, this bunch couldn't be topped.

The sheriff moved to the conclusion of his talk. "Miss Carrie Whiting will be arrivin' on the stage in a little over an hour. Go to the depot, and if you spot anyone who is drunk and disorderly, inform Deputy Curt Weldon. He is there now. I'll be along shortly." He nodded at Rance. "I need to conduct some business with this gentleman first."

"What about?!" The question came from one of the volunteers, who sounded incredulous that any event could be as important as the arrival of Carrie Whiting.

"Well, a hired gun tried to kill this man last night and ended up dead for his efforts. Call me old fashioned, but I believe that is somethin' the local law should take an interest in. Now, get to the depot, all of yuh!"

The four volunteers were far too excited about their duties to be worried about the sheriff's anger. They laughed and patted each other on the back as they scrambled out of the office.

Tal Streeter shook his head. "I tell you, Rance, this whole town has gone loco. Know I wasn't much help to you last night, but the saloons were packed with trouble. The reason the hotel seemed near empty is that everyone was out celebratin'. I didn't hear about the trouble there until—"

"Don't worry about it, Tal. I understand." Dehner moved away from the side wall where he had been leaning but remained on his feet. He was too restless to sit down. "You're only one man, and you only have one full time deputy."

Streeter nodded his head. He was a man of medium height, in his early thirties. He had brown hair and a brown mustache, which looked bushy and neglected.

The lawman pointed at the piles of paper on his desk. "Looked through all the circulars. Can't find no one that matches the description of Holt Conley." The sheriff scrunched up his face and continued, "How many townspeople knew you were comin' to Dry River, Rance?"

"Just you, I guess. I sent you that letter explaining—"

Tal let out a loud curse. "And I left that letter lyin' right here on my desk! This office can get real crowded and hectic sometimes. Anybody could have given it a quick read. This is a small town filled with gossips and, believe me, it ain't jus' the women folk who do the gossipin'. Sorry Rance—"

"Forget it."

"Your job is to help protect Carrie Whiting while she's in Dry River?"

"Yes, that's right. Miss Whiting is based in Dallas, just like the Lowrie Detective Agency, the outfit I work for . . . " Rance paused before continuing. He needed to summarize a meeting that had taken place almost two weeks before. The sheriff could benefit from knowing some of the details. But Dehner couldn't reveal too much of what had been said at that strange meeting in the office of Bertram Lowrie, the founder and head of the Lowrie Detective Agency.

Bertram sat straight in the chair behind his desk looking and sounding every inch a retired officer from the British military. He was tall and thin with white hair and a face dominated by intense gray eyes. Rance Dehner stood beside his boss.

Both men eyed the bald man who sat in front of the desk. He was large and heavy set but not fat.

"It is a pleasure to meet you, Mr. McLeod," Lowrie's delight was genuine. "Your athleticism as a boxer is still the talk of Dallas."

McLeod smirked and looked slightly embarrassed. "I left the squared circle long ago." He pointed toward his nose, which had been broken years before. "Like most pugs, I fought one fight too many."

A cloud was already beginning to form in the room from Lowrie's pipe and McLeod's cigar. Bertram continued to speak in a congenial manner. "I understand that, after you stopped boxing yourself, you began to manage other fighters?"

"Yep. But boxing is . . . well . . . I decided to get more high hat. I started my own theatrical agency."

"And you have come to see us about one of your clients, Miss Carrie Whiting?" Dehner tried to keep his voice casual. Carrie Whiting was fast becoming one of the most famous singers in the United States and all its territories. There had even been rumours of a European tour.

McLeod nodded his head. "I've managed Carrie's career since she was sixteen. I'm the one who came up with calling her the Songbird of the West." He suddenly pointed his cigar at the two men in front of him. "Don't get no crazy notions.

My relationship with Carrie is all proper. I'm sort of the big brother she never had. Carrie needs an agent she can trust and she's got one!"

"Of course, Mr. McLeod, we understand completely." Lowrie fussed with his pipe for a moment, allowing the atmosphere to calm. "Rance Dehner and myself are both very familiar with the career of Carrie Whiting. Please let us know how we can be of service."

George looked down for a moment as if embarrassed by his previous outburst. "There is a certain man in Carrie's life named Skeet Jones."

Bertram Lowrie's response was soft and delicate. "Does Miss Whiting have a romantic interest in Mr. Jones?"

The agent waved his cigar back and forth, dismissing the notion. "No! She hardly ever sees him. I didn't even know the jasper existed until last year when he appeared backstage after one of Carrie's performances here in Dallas. When I first spotted him, I almost tossed him out."

"And why was that?" Following his boss's example, Dehner spoke softly.

McLeod knocked red embers into an ashtray on Lowrie's desk. "I've seen plenty of men like him. They dress like they own a railroad and have smiles wider than a canyon. But you can smell desperation all over them. When Jones told me he was a friend of Carrie's, I laughed in his face. Then Carrie came running out of her dressing room and embraced him. She even cried a bit."

Dehner continued the questioning. "What happened next?"

"Skeet told Carrie he needed to talk with her in private. Carrie invited him into her dressing room. I stayed outside. It seemed longer to me but, according to my timepiece, they were alone together for about fifteen minutes. When they came out Carrie was . . . well . . . she was acting different."

Lowrie's voice remained calm but flames ignited in his eyes. "You must be more specific, Mr. McLeod! What do you mean by 'acting different'?"

George puffed on his cigar as he collected his thoughts. "Carrie was still smiling but she wasn't happy. Her goodbye to Skeet Jones was polite but nothing more. After he left, she gave me an address . . . a hotel room in Dallas . . . and told me to send Jones a cheque for five hundred dollars."

Bertram Lowrie's eyes continued to penetrate through the tobacco smoke that drifted about the room. "Surely you asked her the reason for sending this man so much money?"

"Of course. Carrie told me she owed Skeet Jones. She didn't owe him money, but she owed him. That's all I could get from her."

"Do you suspect blackmail?" Lowrie asked.

McLeod's eyes shifted to the floor. "I don't

know. Carrie has always been very open with me about everything. . . ."

"Everything except Skeet Jones," Dehner added.

George McLeod made a slight nod and said nothing.

Silence followed; Bertram Lowrie cut it short. "If you wish, our agency can do a thorough background check on Mr. Skeet Jones."

"Good idea . . . but you see something else has come up."

Dehner immediately understood what the client was trying to say. "Jones has appeared again, making new demands."

"Not demands exactly." McLeod looked at his cigar without returning it to his mouth. "Skeet Jones now owns a saloon in Dry River. He's asked Carrie to sing there. She's agreed."

"How did Jones contact Miss Whiting?" Dehner asked.

McLeod shook his head. "Don't know. Mail maybe. Carrie just informed me yesterday that she would be leaving for Dry River in two weeks." The agent gave a bitter laugh. "Next month, she's opening in New York. But first she's going to play Dry River, Texas."

"As I understand it, you want us to do a background check on this character who is bothering Miss Whiting. How else can we be of help?"

A businessman himself, George McLeod

understood that Lowrie was trying to keep him on point. Still, he had trouble articulating his thoughts. "Carrie is determined to go ahead with singing in this jasper's saloon. But the whole affair has her jittery and worried. She hasn't been herself lately."

McLeod grimaced before continuing. "Guess I haven't been myself either. I will accompany Carrie on the trip to Dry River. Once there, I will stick as close to her as I can." The agent shifted in his chair, then faced Lowrie directly. "I want you to send a man to Dry River, have him look around and see what, if any, danger Carrie might be in. He's to remain in Dry River until Carrie and I leave."

"Is he to remain secret about his purpose of being in town?" Lowrie was now taking notes.

"No. No need for that. I want your man to check in with me regularly. I may want some help in guarding Carrie."

Excitement charged through Rance Dehner. He was about to get an assignment guarding one of the most beautiful women in the nation. He swallowed and tried to keep the expression on his face business-like.

Sheriff Tal Streeter smiled and laughed gently. "So, Skeet Jones really does know Carrie Whiting. Have to fess up I didn't quite believe him, even when he claimed she was arrivin' on today's stage. Good thing he's tellin' the truth. We have folks here from miles around."

Dehner returned the smile, confident he had told the lawman what he needed to know. "Another thing we have to keep in mind. Holt Conley trying to kill me last night may not be related to the whole Carrie Whiting matter. I've made a lot of enemies. Conley could have been connected with a past case. Still, I think there is a connection. Like I told you last night, Conley's dying words could only have been about the singer—"

The door to the office banged open and Deputy Curt Weldon ran inside. He was in his mid-twenties, lean, muscular, and very worried.

Tal Streeter read the concern on his deputy's face. "What is it?"

"Matt Roberts just rode in from his farm. Says he spotted the stagecoach, the one bringin' Carrie Whiting."

"So?"

"Outlaws stopped the coach. They have it surrounded."

Chapter Five

Carrie Whiting sat alone in the passenger section of the stagecoach. Well, sort of alone. George McLeod was dozing on the seat across from hers. But even when he was awake George understood Carrie's need to retreat into her own thoughts.

The solitude was bliss. Of course, the ride would be over soon and she would once again have to be . . . well . . . Carrie Whiting, the Songbird of the West. People would expect her to be bubbly and smiling and, of course, everyone would demand *just a few minutes of your time.*

She glanced at the passing landscape and admonished herself for the self-pity. Carrie Whiting was blessed and knew it. She was, as several newspaper reviewers described her, "a fine figure of a woman." Carrie had long blond hair, a beautiful face and a voice equally beautiful. "Be grateful for your blessings," she whispered to herself.

The young woman closed her eyes and reflected on the fact that all of her blessings had almost landed her in a living nightmare. Skeet Jones had rescued her. She owed him. But Skeet was a complicated man and time had changed him. She would have to tell Skeet that singing in his saloon was the last payment on her debt. How would he take it?

The Songbird of the West began to doze lightly. She had a fragment of a dream where she was singing in a third rate saloon as men viciously gunned each other down. Suddenly, the men stopped killing each other and began to aim their guns at her.

Gunshots yanked Carrie from her dream. The stagecoach lurched forward at a faster speed. From above she could hear the shotgun returning fire. The sound of hoof beats pounding behind the stagecoach drew closer.

George McLeod was awake and aiming a pistol out the window of the stagecoach; he cursed as he fired his first shot. "This damn coach is hopping like a scared rabbit. I can't get off a good shot."

The young woman had to brace herself with both arms in order to not bounce around the rocking and swaying coach. She could hear shouts of "Pull over!" coming from the outlaws.

Horsemen appeared on both sides of the coach at almost the same time. The horses moved with fast, graceful strides. For a fleeting moment, the scene looked choreographed, like one of the dance numbers Carrie performed in theaters.

That illusion was quickly shattered by more gunfire and curses from the shotgun. Shouts of "OK, OK!" finally came from the driver.

As the stagecoach slowed to a halt, a rifle plunged past the coach's window and hit the ground like a dead bird. The shotgun had followed an order given in pantomime.

A loud threatening voice sounded from one of the outlaws. "Mister, toss out your gun now. I'm warning yuh. If yuh cause any trouble at all, I kill the woman."

McLeod grimaced, tossed his Remington out the window and whispered to Carrie. "We'll give these crooks all the money that's on us. That'll be the end of it."

The outlaw who had spoken dismounted and opened the passenger door. He pointed his gun at George McLeod. "You, out, right now!"

The agent hurried out of the coach and provided no resistance as the crook jerked the wallet out of his suit pocket. "That is all the money the woman and I are carrying," George said. "You can leave her alone."

The outlaw gave a fake sigh of remorse. "Ah now, don't make a few lonely jaspers pass up the chance to meet Carrie Whiting. Step outta the coach, Miss Whiting."

Carrie felt a new tension as she followed the instructions. She was beginning to doubt her agent's earlier assertion. This seemed like a lot more than a hold up.

Her eyes quickly scanned the situation. There were four robbers, all of whom were now on one side of the coach with guns drawn. Three were still on horseback. The man who had dismounted was still pointing his gun at George McLeod. All of the crooks had bandannas covering the bottom half of their faces. Their eyes gleamed with wicked amusement.

Another horseman approached the stagecoach. Carrie hoped this might be help. Her hope was short lived as she saw that the newcomer was masked and guiding a riderless horse.

"Get on the horse, lady!" The speaker shifted his gun from McLeod to her.

The young woman chose defiance. "And just what will happen if I decide not to get on the horse?"

Carrie realized immediately that she had made a tragic mistake. The gunman gave a cold laugh then turned to one of his mounted companions who held a six shooter pointed at the shotgun and the driver. "Let's show Miss Carrie Whiting what happens when she don't act nice."

"Okay, boss," The outlaw opened fire. A hail of bullets penetrated both men sitting on the stagecoach bench. They dropped from the stagecoach onto the ground.

Carrie screamed, as George McLeod embraced her. "There was no reason to do that," the agent shouted. "You shot those men down in cold blood."

"If the lady hadn't been so disagreeable, we might have let one of them live."

Anger still resounded in the agent's voice. "What are you talking about?"

"Yuh step away from the girl and I'll explain it to yuh real simple like."

McLeod took two steps away from Carrie. The outlaw slammed a pistol against George's head. The agent staggered but was able to keep his balance. With a hard kick, the outlaw tripped McLeod who slammed face first against the ground.

Carrie screamed and yelled at the outlaw to stop.

"Shut up!" The order came from one of the horsemen, who pointed his pistol directly at the singer. "I ain't never killt a woman, and I'd kinda like to know what it feels like."

The outlaw who was on his feet pressed his six gun against the back of McLeod's head. "We're about to begin us some important business talks. Yuh need to know we're real serious. We jus' killed two men and we've already killed a ranch owner and his wife. Yuh can't get hung twice. We got nothin' to lose by killing Miss Carrie Whiting. That'll give yuh somethin' to sleep on."

The outlaw again slammed his gun against George McLeod's head, this time knocking him out.

"That'll keep the jasper for a while. He'll have

a real interesting story to tell when the law gets here."

The outlaw then looked mockingly at Carrie. "Get on the horse, Miss Whiting. This is the last time I'm gonna ask yuh polite like."

Carrie got on the horse.

Chapter Six

Rance Dehner and the two lawmen from Dry River reined up beside the stagecoach. They quickly dismounted and checked the bodies that lay on the ground.

"You can't help those men. They're both dead." The grim words came from George McLeod, who leaned against the stagecoach holding a handkerchief against his head.

The three newcomers formed a half circle around the agent. As they did, Dehner felt the surge of helplessness and anger that always plagued him when he arrived at a scene too late.

The detective took a deep breath and brought his emotions under control. He spoke quickly to the sheriff and his deputy, "This man is George McLeod, Carrie Whiting's agent. He was travelling with her." He switched his gaze back to McLeod. "Are you OK? Can you tell us what happened?"

"Yep. One varmint hit me in the head with his gun. Hell, I've fought boxers who could do more damage with their fists. . . ." McLeod then gave a concise, factual account of the hold up.

"Did any of the outlaws say anything that could

indicate where they have taken Miss Whiting?" Dehner asked.

All four men were struggling to remain calm. As he spoke it was obvious McLeod was having more trouble than most. "I've been thinking over every word those bastards said. Thank God, one of 'em was stupid as a donkey. He bragged about killing a rancher and his wife. Reckon it coulda been for horses, but more likely they wanted to hide Carrie at the ranch."

"That ties in!" Deputy Curt Weldon shouted.

"What do you mean?" Dehner asked.

"Yesterday, Sunday afternoon, I was jawin' with Hiram Peterson; he owns Peterson's Restaurant. Hiram tole me that Bert and Patricia Kimball didn't come into town on Saturday to pick up supplies and eat at the restaurant like they usually do. The Kimballs always look forward to Saturdays and gettin' away from that ten head ranch of—"

"Do the Kimballs have hired hands?" Dehner interjected.

The deputy shook his head. "Can't afford help. Live by themselfs on the ranch."

Dehner's voice gained intensity. "Do either one of you lawmen know where the Kimball ranch is?"

"Sure, I've been there a lot, let's check it out—now!" The sheriff's voice sounded like an order.

George McLeod gave a quick, indifferent look

46

at the red stains on his handkerchief, then stuffed it into his coat pocket. "I'll unhitch one of the horses from the stage. I can ride without a saddle. I'm coming with you."

As the men mounted their horses, Dehner spotted vultures forming undulating black circles in the sky. In a decent world the bodies of the stagecoach driver and the shotgun would be taken into town immediately and spared the ravages of vultures and coyotes.

But the world was far from decent. They would retrieve the bodies when they could. The four men rode off.

Chapter Seven

The sun had set as the four men approached a tall, wide knoll. "I think we should leave the horses here," Tal said. "We can hoof it up to the top of the hill. From there we'll get a good view of the Kimball ranch. What there is of it."

The foursome quickly dismounted and tied up at a grove of trees. Rance removed field glasses from his saddle bags and a Winchester from its scabbard. The men moved quietly up the knoll. At the top they lay on the ground and studied the scene below. There was a small house sided by a corral. The house faced a barn which, like the rest of the ranch, appeared modest but well cared for.

"There are a lot of little ranches like this 'round here," Tal whispered to Dehner. The sheriff was situated between his deputy and the detective. George McLeod was on Dehner's other side. "Ten head operations, they sell cattle to the larger outfits. I think the Kimballs sold their herd a few weeks ago. Ain't started a new one yet, though I reckon there could be some calves around somewhere."

"I'm just hoping the Kimballs are still alive," Dehner focused the glasses on the house below.

A kerosene light flickered from the front window; it appeared to be struggling for survival against a dark night bereft of stars or a moon.

Three men stepped out of the house, one of them carrying a lantern. They untied the horses from the hitch rail and began to lead them into the barn. Dehner watched them closely.

"We're at the right place," Dehner whispered. "Those jaspers have the look of hired guns."

"Should we rush them now?" Curt Weldon asked as he drummed his fingers on the barrel of his Henry. "This might be a good time, while three of them are in the barn seein' after the horses."

Tal shook his head. "I'm just a small town sheriff. Ain't had much experience with kidnappin's. But we need to be real careful here. Make sure we know exactly where the girl is."

The deputy's eyebrows shot up. "You don't think Carrie Whiting is in the house?"

Anger came into Streeter's voice but he still spoke in a whisper. "Yes, she's in the house, but where? Our first job is to get her back safe. If we rush the place, one of those owlhoots could have a gun to her head in no time."

Dehner nodded, "What do you have in mind, Tal?"

"I've visited this ranch many times. Bert and Patricia are friends of mine." The sheriff paused for a moment. His face went gray. "Or they

50

were. Anyhow, I'm goin' to move around back. The way I see it these thugs plan on askin' for a ransom. If they get the money, they'll free the girl. That means they have to take precautions."

"What kind of precautions?" Weldon asked.

"The money will probably come from Dallas." Tal continued to study the ranch below him as he spoke. "That means they need to hold Carrie Whiting captive for a few days. You can bet they don't want her to see or even hear them much. And they sure don't want her escapin' out a window."

Dehner got the point. "They will keep the woman prisoner in a room that's boarded up."

"Exactly," Streeter replied. "And the Kimballs have windows in every room of their three room house." He pointed straight down. "You can see the front window for the livin' area. In the back is a large window which looks into the kitchen. There's nothin' separatin' the kitchen from the livin' room. So, it don't seem likely they'd put the girl in that area. On the far side of the house is the window for the bedroom. I'll bet the bedroom window is boarded up and that is where Carrie Whiting is at. But we gotta make sure."

"Do you have a plan, Sheriff?" McLeod asked.

"My deputy and I will sneak down. There's two owlhoots in the house right now. Curt and I will handle them. I'm hopin' you and Rance can hold off those gunslicks in the barn. After Curt and I start down, wait a few minutes, then make your way down to the barn. There'll be shootin' comin' from the house. The jaspers in the barn will come runnin' out to help. That's when you take them prisoner or kill 'em."

"We'll handle our part; good luck," Dehner said. The sheriff drew his six shooter as he quietly got up and made his way down to the ranch. His deputy followed, carrying the Henry.

Dehner watched the lawmen through his field glasses but not for long. "Can't see them anymore," Rance whispered to McLeod as he put the glasses down. "We'll do what the sheriff told us and give them a few minutes before we move."

Time passed; the detective didn't even try to guess at how much. The tense circumstances made an accurate assessment impossible.

"I can't take any more of this waiting," McLeod's whisper was laced with desperation. Dehner realized the agent had been controlling some powerful emotions. That control was about to break.

"It's about time for us to move." Dehner hoped he was right.

Rance put down his field glasses and picked up the Winchester. McLeod yanked his Remington from a shoulder holster. The detective led as both men made their way down the knoll.

A whirl of scattering gravel sounded behind

Rance. He turned and saw George McLeod performing a frantic dance. The agent had stumbled and was trying to keep his balance. His right arm propelled into the air and he fired a bullet into the sky.

Dehner looked downward and thought he saw two shadows emerge from the barn. His uncertainty was quickly shattered. McLeod followed his shot with a loud curse and one of the outlaws fired in McLeod's direction. The agent stumbled again and this time, fell. Dehner squeezed off a shot at the flash of red which had cut the night from below.

A man's cry of pain joined the sound of gunfire as another red explosion launched from the bottom of the knoll. Dehner hit the ground, returned fire and missed. Instinctively, his target snapped two shots at the detective. The shooter's flames telegraphed his location. Rance's third shot took the outlaw down.

Dehner cautiously sprang to his feet and moved to where George McLeod lay on the ground. "Have you been hit?"

"No, the shot only threw me off balance. I had already stumbled over my own two feet." Like Dehner, McLeod kept his voice low. But the anger he felt with himself was there. "Sorry."

"Never mind." Dehner spoke as he reloaded. "We have to check on those two outlaws. Make sure they're really out of action."

The two men proceeded quietly down the knoll, guns in hand. They found two bodies lying on the ground. Both were dead. Dehner glanced toward the house. The shots must have alerted the remaining kidnappers that their hideout had been discovered. But the detective couldn't spot any movement from that direction.

Hoof beats pounded from behind the barn. George McLeod fired a shot at the blur of a horse and rider before it vanished into the darkness.

"The snake got away, damn!" McLeod shouted.

"Keep your voice down!" Dehner ordered in a stage whisper. "Tal forgot to tell us the barn has back doors, guess there were horses—"

An explosion of gunshots came from the house. "Tal and Curt may be in trouble," Dehner said. "Let's move."

As the two men approached the house, they could see that at least some of the gunshots were coming from inside. They cautiously circled around to the back which, as Streeter had indicated, had one large window. The curtains were open and one of the two shutters had broken off; the other was wide open. Dehner peered inside while George McLeod moved to check the far side.

After a few moments, the agent returned, crouching near the window. "What do you see?"

The detective was already in a crouch under the window. He took another careful look. Dehner had long ago trained himself to observe every detail of a scene. He flattened himself against the house before answering McLeod's question. "The only light comes from a lamp on a table by the front window. Curt Weldon is lying on the floor, right under the kitchen window. His rifle is lying in the middle of the floor. There's a path of blood leading to his body. I think Tal dragged him there and I think Weldon's alive."

Dehner paused for a moment as if expressing doubt about his last statement. He inhaled quickly and continued. "There's a bureau pulled out from the wall near the front door, with a gunman behind it. The other kidnapper is lying on the floor. I don't know if he's dead or alive. Streeter is in the kitchen. His only protection is a kitchen table he's knocked over. The jasper behind the bureau and Streeter fire at each other sporadically. Neither man has been able to take down the other and neither one can get to Curt's Henry. They are both trapped where they are."

McLeod nodded his head. "The window on the other side of the house is boarded up. That's where they have Carrie, all right."

Dehner handed McLeod the Winchester and duck walked away from the back window. "I'm going around and enter the house by the front door. Pay a surprise visit on our friend behind the bureau."

"Why? We could smoke him from here."

Another volley of shots sounded from inside the house. Dehner wondered how much ammo each man had left. "I want to take one man alive. That owlhoot lying on the floor is probably dead."

"What's the big deal about taking a prisoner? These jaspers are real snakes."

"Yep," Dehner agreed. "But they're hired guns. Carrie Whiting won't be safe until we find out who hired them."

The two men exchanged nods as George McLeod took a position by the window and Dehner scooted around to the front of the house. As he carefully stepped onto the front porch the detective realized he had to keep low. When Tal Streeter saw a man coming through the door, he might assume it was one of the outlaws who had been in the barn.

Colt .45 in hand, the detective crouched down on the porch and opened the front door. He was now only a few feet from a lanky outlaw whose entire body pivoted quickly to greet the newcomer.

"Drop the gun." Dehner ordered.

"I was about to say the same thing to you, stranger." The gunman pointed his six shooter directly at Dehner. "I guess we got us what they call a stand off."

"All your pals are dead, mister," Dehner said. "Even if you kill me, there are lawmen all around this place."

The gunman laughed derisively. "Well, there is one less lawman. I just shot your friend in the kitchen."

As he pretended to look toward the kitchen, Dehner fired, a quick second before his adversary could pull the trigger. The bullet entered the outlaw's shoulder. He slammed against the bureau, his arm flailing out and tossing his gun a few feet away. Instinctively, the outlaw began to scramble for the weapon. He was stopped by a bullet from Streeter's Colt double action revolver.

The sheriff quickly ran toward Dehner, motioning with his gun at the man he had just killed. "This gunney won't cause us no more problems. What about the three jaspers in the barn?"

"Two are dead, the other got away. How's Curt?"

The sheriff looked confused, as if he needed to take some immediate action but couldn't think of what it was. "The gunshots from the barn smartened those thugs up fast. They spotted us out back and opened fire. Curt killed one of them. The other seemed to run for the front door. Curt charged in through the kitchen window. I had to follow him. The kid got creased in the noggin and went down. I moved him to where he'd be sort of safe. By that time, the outlaw was behind the desk. I was gettin' low on ammo. Good thing yuh came along."

Streeter's hands were shaking. The lawman seemed to be experiencing the jitters as well as the exhaustion-excitement that follows a life threatening encounter. Dehner understood the reaction.

"Hey guys," George McLeod shouted from behind them. He had come in through the window. "Don't we have one more job to do here?" He pointed at the door to the room where Carrie was being held prisoner.

Tal Streeter laughed and ran a hand over his head. "Knew we had come here to do somethin'."

Chapter Eight

Rance Dehner felt nervous and apprehensive. He stood erect and held his breath. There was an explosion of smoke followed by loud cheering.

Dehner was standing on a small platform in the Silver Crown saloon. The platform was located a few feet from the bar. With Rance were Tal Streeter, Curt Weldon, George McLeod and Carrie Whiting. Of the foursome, only Carrie appeared relaxed. That didn't surprise Dehner. Carrie Whiting would be quite used to being in front of people and having her picture taken.

A lean man of average height, wearing a brown suit and derby, jumped onto the stage. He had been introduced earlier to Dehner as Felix Murphy, the town mayor. Murphy smiled at the large crowd in front of him. Today, the saloon was being turned into a theater for a few hours. The tables had been stacked along the side walls and the chairs set up in rows. There were a large number of women and children present.

"Thank you, Glenn," the mayor addressed the man who had just taken the picture. Glenn Wilson was the photographer, reporter and editor of the local paper. "Glenn tells me that the picture he just took and the story of what happened to Miss Whiting yesterday will go all over the country and really put our town on the map!"

There was another round of loud cheering. Felix used the moment to whisper instructions to Carrie's rescuers. "You gents can vamoose off the stage now."

The four men hurried back to the front row, where they had seats of honor sitting with Skeet Jones, the owner of the Silver Crown. Jones was a tall, dark haired man in his late twenties. Dehner had known him for less than a day, but he totally agreed with McLeod's description of the bar owner as a desperate con man.

After they sat down, Dehner spoke in a low voice to the sheriff, who was sitting on his left side. "This must be tough on you. At least we found where those snakes buried the bodies of the Kimballs . . . seems kind of odd to be having a town wide celebration."

Tal Streeter smiled whimsically. "The West is a brutal place. Yuh have to take your pleasures where yuh can find 'em. I don't blame folks. I'm jus' grateful Curt wasn't really hurt bad . . . doc says that bandage on his head can come off soon, probably—"

Streeter stopped talking as Felix Murphy's voice boomed over the room. "I see a lot of unfamiliar faces here today," He chuckled nervously before continuing, "I want to welcome all of our visitors and encourage you all to come back to Dry River. This town has so much to offer—"

A shout came from the crowd. "Yep. We got us a lotta dust and hot sun."

Felix pretended to be amused by the remark. He allowed the laughter to subside, then carried on. "As all of you know, Miss Carrie Whiting will be giving a performance here at the Silver Crown tomorrow night and the night after. At those performances, liquor will be served. Today, she is giving a matinee for all the families of Dry River and places beyond." He turned to face Carrie who was standing beside him. "Miss Whiting, speaking on behalf—"

This time the shouter sounded angry. "Enough, Felix! Nobody came here to listen to you!"

"Ah, yes." The mayor hastily pulled a card from his side pocket and began to read from it. "Ladies and gentlemen, girls and boys, Mr. Skeet Jones is pleased to bring to our fine town, the musical artistry of Miss Carrie Whiting!" Murphy joined the group in the front row.

Loud applause and several whistles came from the audience. Carrie bowed gracefully, nodded at the pianist positioned at the opposite side of the platform from the bar and began to sing.

Dehner was totally captivated by Carrie's performance. This was a much different Carrie Whiting he was seeing. The previous day, Carrie had been relieved and very grateful when rescued from the kidnappers. But she had also been withdrawn and quiet. During the picture taking, Carrie had been poised and gracious but still distant. Now, she seemed totally alive, connecting with her audience and reveling in the moment.

The singer seemed to be sending out her magnificent smiles to the children in the audience. Carrie seemed especially joyful at the end of the concert when she led the audience in a rousing sing along of *Oh! Susanna*.

As the singer took her bows, Dehner began to chuckle at his own pretentions. Why fool himself by trying to think like a theater critic? He was as dazzled by Carrie Whiting as everyone else,—especially the males in the audience.

Skeet Jones jumped onto the platform and immediately placed an arm around Carrie Whiting. He tried to shout over the applause. "Remember men, Carrie will be back here for two nights. For that matter, you'll be seeing her a lot at saloons owned by Skeet Jones!"

Felix Murphy jumped up from his chair and declared loudly. "Before we all go to dinner, let's hear a round of applause for Skeet Jones, the man who brought Carrie Whiting to our town!"

Carrie's name ginned up the applause. While the clapping continued, Skeet kept his arm around the singer, escorting her off the stage. The saloon owner made a very wide beckoning gesture and a short, pudgy man ran toward him. He was wearing a battered derby with the brim hanging loose, a faded red shirt and shiny brown pants.

"Laszlow, we're in for a busy night. Get those tables back in place and do it pronto!"

"Yes sir, Mr. Jones!" Laszlo hastened off to do what he was told.

Skeet smiled at Carrie. He seemed to be trying to impress her with his exalted status: a man who gave orders that were quickly obeyed. Carrie's face exuded anger, not admiration.

Jones didn't seem to notice. He guided the young woman past the bar and through an open doorway. Dehner moved toward that doorway and saw that it led to a small corridor with a room at the end, presumably an office. Jones swished Carrie Whiting into that room.

People were beginning to leave the Silver Crown and head out for a place to eat. Inside the saloon, men were milling about as Laszlo set up for a busy night.

Dehner eased into the corridor, partially closing the door to conceal himself. He moved close to the office door, which was shut. Carrie Whiting had not been kidnapped again but Dehner still believed she was in danger.

"No more cheap tricks like you just pulled!" Carrie broke loose from Jones's arm the moment they entered his large office. "Two more performances and the debt will be paid in full, Skeet."

Jones gave the woman a bland smile and gestured with both hands as if haggling over prices with a supplier. "The booze business can bring in riches. I mean big money. The key is volume. One saloon can bring in loot, but owning a lot of saloons, well, let me tell you, that'll buy you the finest house in Dallas or Denver."

"So?"

"I'm gonna own saloons all over the west, Carrie, and you're going to sing in them. You can tour around—"

"No Skeet, like I said, after the next two nights my relationship with you is over!"

Jones's smile widened. He took a few strides that placed him behind the office's one desk. Carrie Whiting had been in show business long enough to recognize a dramatic build up but she was still shocked by what happened next.

Skeet opened the top drawer of the desk and brought out a very small box which he held in his right palm. He opened it slowly revealing a diamond ring. "Carrie, we'd make a great team. Let's you and me get hitched. We'll have a big wedding in Dallas, with—"

Despite herself, Carrie Whiting broke out laughing. She turned and walked toward the door. She had her laughter under control when she stopped and faced the saloon owner. "You don't want a wife, Skeet. You want to be rich and important, a man everyone looks up to. Nothing wrong with that, but you'll have to earn it yourself. I'm not doing it for you."

The Songbird of the West pressed her lips together and briefly looked down. She regretted her laughter. The young woman returned her gaze to Skeet Jones, who was still standing behind his desk. "I'm grateful for what you did for me, Skeet. But the road has run both ways. I helped you with money to buy this saloon, and that crowd that was there tonight didn't get in for free. The next two appearances will bring in more money. After that, it will be time for us to go our separate ways."

Carrie had taken another step toward the door when Jones grabbed her by the arm and pulled her toward him. Passion steamed from his eyes like heat from a branding iron.

"Skeet, please, let me go."

"You think you're too good for me. You've outgrown the low life who rescued you from a whorehouse. Well, let me tell you—"

Rance Dehner flung the door open and stepped inside, "You've talked enough, Mr. Jones. Let Miss Whiting go."

"I don't take orders from some two bit detective. Get out of my office!"

"I will. But first you're going to let go of Miss Whiting."

Jones yanked the young woman behind him and lunged at Dehner. The saloon owner was too angry to fight well. He telegraphed his first punch, which Rance easily ducked. Dehner's first punch sent Skeet Jones to the floor.

"I've been listening outside," Dehner spoke in a monotone to his opponent, who was slowly getting up. "I'm sure Miss Whiting is willing to forget this encounter. I suggest you do the same."

On his feet, Skeet Jones leaned against his desk, this time for support, "Get out. Both of you!"

Dehner gently took Carrie Whiting by the arm and guided her out of the office. Matters did not get any easier when they got to the boardwalk. A crowd of people began to gather around the singer. Carrie quickly whispered into Dehner's ear, "Could you get me to Peterson's Restaurant? I have a room reserved for supper there."

Carrie then began to chat it up with her fans, thanking them for their compliments. Dehner quickly understood the role he had been assigned. He was the bad guy. He had to say things like, "Excuse us please, Miss Whiting needs to eat supper, just like the rest of us," as he guided Carrie toward the restaurant.

At the restaurant, the owner, Hiram Peterson, greeted them. He was a middle aged, pleasant appearing man who beamed at Carrie but appeared uncertain about her companion. Dehner figured Skeet Jones had made the arrangements and Hiram expected Jones to be escorting the star.

The owner maintained his courteous demeanor as he escorted Carrie and Rance across the restaurant. They passed the kitchen to arrive at a back door which Hiram opened in a ceremonious manner. "This room is not up to the standards of Dallas, Miss Whiting, but I hope you will enjoy your meal here."

"Oh, this is wonderful!" Carrie exclaimed. "Thank you for going to so much trouble."

Hiram's face turned a happy red. "My pleasure, Miss Whiting."

Dehner was able to hide his amusement. Hiram had done a fine job of transforming a storage room into a private dining area. He had run a long, thin piece of wood across the ceiling of the room. The wood served as a curtain rod. The curtain itself was black and blocked the view of most of the room. The dining table was round with a white tablecloth. In the middle of the table was a small green vase containing a red rose. The table was sitting on a hastily cut piece of red carpet.

"I will be bringing your food shortly, Miss Whiting!" Hiram hurried off.

Carrie looked about in an appreciative manner. "I feel guilty putting Mr. Peterson to all of this trouble. But I really do need a private room to eat in. Otherwise . . . well . . . you saw how people can be."

Dehner remained standing in the doorway while Carrie stood by the table. "I sure did. But it was a pleasure escorting you here. Enjoy your evening meal, Miss Whiting. I'll be right outside if you need me."

"Wait a minute, Mr. Dehner, you can't expect a girl to dine alone. You must join me."

"Ah . . . I hadn't . . ."

A playful look appeared on the singer's face. "After all, you are supposed to watch over me. So, come in and watch."

Dehner stepped in and closed the door behind him.

Chapter Nine

Carrie Whiting was obviously amused by her companion's nervousness. She smiled mischievously as Dehner held the singer's chair for her and then sat down across from her.

There was a light knock on the door. Hiram and a young man he introduced as his eleven year old son, Clayton, marched in carrying dishes and a tray of food. Carrie once again beamed with delight over the service and paid special attention to the boy. Clayton could only smile and nod, his face reflecting shyness and adoration. Dehner realized that the boy would remember this night for a very long time to come.

Once Hiram and his son departed and the couple began eating, the detective wanted to exude charm and wit but found himself unable to do so. He settled for discussing business. "I heard your conversation with Skeet Jones."

Carrie responded with a mirthless grin.

Dehner continued, "Do you think Jones arranged the kidnapping? He seems to be a man who always needs money."

The singer shook her head. "I don't think so . . . but I can't be sure . . ."

Carrie paused, trying to collect her thoughts.

"Skeet can't keep his emotions in check. His pride gets the best of him. To use a theatrical term, that is Skeet Jones's fatal flaw."

"You should have been a detective, Miss Whiting."

The singer laughed and the playful expression returned to her face. "I couldn't have been nearly as good a detective as you, Mr. Dehner. I know more about you than you think."

The detective raised his eyebrows and looked curious.

"I spend a lot of time alone," the singer continued. "Private compartments on trains, hotel rooms, what have you. So, I do a lot of reading. Your name appears occasionally in the newspapers, Rance Dehner."

"I try to avoid that."

"I know," Carrie's voice maintained its playful quality. "The name 'Rance Dehner' always appears far down in the article. If there is a local lawman involved, he always gets the credit. I'm afraid your shyness disqualifies you for a career in the theater, Mr. Dehner."

Dehner needed to move the conversation in a more serious direction. "Right now, my career involves protecting you and I can't do that very well without more information. What is this debt you owe to Skeet Jones?"

Carrie took a small bite of food as the playfulness left her eyes. Dehner was sorry to see it go.

"I have found this hard to talk about. I only confided the truth to George just before we came here." The singer spoke as she returned the fork to her plate. "I was born in Calhoun Texas, an only child. My parents were good, God-fearing people. We went to church every Sunday. I loved the music, and started singing solos in church when I was nine."

Carrie paused and inhaled before continuing. "I was a very naive child. The town had one brothel, called Bob's Place. I was intrigued by it because I occasionally heard music coming from inside. A piano would be playing and sometimes I could hear a woman singing."

"You must have heard the same thing coming from saloons."

The woman nodded her head. "Yes, but there was such rowdiness at the saloons: men shouting curses and staggering outside drunk. There didn't seem to be any of that coming from Bob's. I thought it was a wonderful place where people went to enjoy music, sort of like a theater."

Both Rance and his companion went silent for a moment, reflecting on the hard reality always waiting to shatter childhood innocence. Carrie continued in a low voice. "Both of my parents were killed in an accident when I was twelve. I had to go live with an aunt and uncle."

"I'm sorry."

"Thank you. I was miserable living with my

relatives. They were very poor and had five kids of their own. I was a burden on them and they let me know it."

"What did you do?" Dehner asked.

"I thought I could support myself by being a singer. I ran off and went to Bob's Place. I walked in on a Thursday morning. Not much going on and Bob was happy to talk with me."

"I'll bet he was."

Carrie gave a caustic smile to Dehner's remark. "Bob Hoover told me I could live there and all I had to do was sing and be nice to the customers."

"And you had no idea what he meant by 'be nice to the customers.' "

"None. I was so naive! Bob Hoover made me feel important. He bought me a new dress and even gave me what he called a stage name— Angela the Angel. He told me that on my opening night at Bob's Place I would be introduced to the most important man in town, a wealthy rancher named Jack Sather."

Carrie Whiting gave Rance a detailed account of what happened on the night of her first appearance at Bob's Place. The singer emphasized that Skeet Jones had shot Jack Sather in self defense but had to leave Calhoun to escape retribution for killing the town's most powerful man. At the time, she was terrified and willingly went with him.

"What happened after you left Calhoun?"

"Skeet did what he said he was going to do," Carrie answered. "We stopped at a nearby ranch, he bought a horse for me and we rode to Dallas. Skeet was aware of my . . . innocence . . . and, well, he was a complete gentleman."

Something special came into the woman's eyes as she recalled the Skeet Jones she had once known. "To make a long story short," she continued, "we ended up stopping at a small church right outside of Dallas. The pastor is named Reverend Craig Barton. He and his wife Emma agreed to take me in. They live in a house next door to the church. Skeet promised to visit me often."

"Did he keep that promise?"

The look in Carrie's eyes changed to something between sadness and confusion. "Yes, and I welcomed those visits . . . at first."

The woman stopped speaking. Dehner needed to prod her on. "But Skeet Jones began to change."

"Yes. He began to show up with alcohol on his breath and bragging about how rich and successful he was. One day he barged into the house laughing and waving money he had won in a poker game, or he claimed that's how he got it. Anyhow, he wanted me to go with him—"

Dehner interrupted, "Go with him where?"

"Skeet didn't say. Only claimed he was going

to buy me a mansion. By this time, I was fifteen and a lot wiser. I said no and Skeet began to yell at me. Reverend Barton got in between us and ordered Skeet out of the house. Skeet refused and they began to argue. The argument went on for some time and Skeet became more and more threatening. Finally, he pulled a gun on Reverend Barton, grabbed my arm and forced me to go with him."

Carrie sighed deeply and closed her eyes. "As we went out the door, he whispered to me, 'Remember the last time we rode off together?' He seemed to be trying to win me over. In a way, I pitied him."

"Where did he take you?"

The singer smiled and shook her head. "Not far past the front porch of the house. During all the commotion, Emma had gone for the law. A deputy sheriff was waiting outside. He took away Skeet's gun and beat him up good. I got the impression Skeet and the deputy had crossed paths before. Skeet never came to the Barton home again."

"George McLeod told me about the visit Jones paid on you after a concert in Dallas last year. Was that the first time you had seen Skeet since you watched the deputy beat him up?"

"Yes," Carrie said. "I had hoped he was once again the Skeet Jones who had rescued me from the brothel. Guess I am still pretty naive. Skeet needed money to help him buy a saloon. I gave it to him."

Carrie picked up her fork and dabbled at her food without eating it. Moisture was forming in her eyes as she again faced Dehner. "Skeet did me a great favor when he saved me from the brothel, but I think he hurt himself."

"How so?"

Carrie's speech slowed as if she were carefully reviewing facts. "That night, Skeet outdrew a tough looking ramrod, and then killed Jack Sather, the most important person in the town. And he got away with it! I think he came away from that night with a crazy notion of being a big man, a very important person."

Dehner nodded his head. "How did Reverend Barton and his wife treat you?"

"Wonderful! Mrs. Barton is skilled in music. She taught me piano and helped with my singing. They are both doing well. I visit them often. They are happy for me but concerned at the same time."

Playfulness returned to Carrie's face. "Now, it is time for me to question you, sir! Tell me, how many damsels in distress have you rescued?"

A look of sharp pain flashed over Dehner's face. He quickly recovered and copied his companion's playful tone. "Well, I had a hand in rescuing the Songbird of the West. Such a very special damsel is enough for any man to rescue."

The conversation continued to be light and the rest of the evening passed far too quickly. Dehner realized that young Clayton was not the only one who would long remember this very special dinner.

As they were walking to the hotel, Dehner filled Carrie in on his assignment. "George McLeod has the room to the left of yours. I am your neighbor on the right."

"I believe in being a good neighbor," Carrie said as they approached the hotel.

Dehner wondered exactly what she meant by that or if she meant anything at all. His musings were quickly cut short. Once inside the hotel lobby, Carrie Whiting again became the Songbird of the West, granting everyone a few minutes of her complete attention.

Twenty minutes later, the pair arrived at Carrie Whiting's room. The singer leaned against the door and gave her escort a whimsical smile. "I very much enjoyed this evening."

"I'll bet you say that to all your body guards."

"Tonight I really mean it. I suspect you and I have a lot in common, Rance Dehner."

"And how is that, Carrie Whiting?"

"We are both trapped by our jobs. A singing career makes for a very lonely, isolated existence. But I wouldn't want to change. There are such special rewards in what I do. I suspect that being a detective is much the same way."

Dehner experienced a tornado of emotions, all of which he kept in check. But his will power was eroding. His voice wavered a bit, "Good night, Miss Whiting."

"Good night, Mr. Dehner."

The detective tried not to look behind him as he scooted next door to his room. He stepped inside, his mind full of vivid pictures of his evening with the Songbird of the West.

Those pictures were shattered by a piercing scream.

Chapter Ten

Dehner raced into the hallway. The door to Carrie's room was closed but not locked. As he charged inside, Rance saw the singer standing against a side wall staring with terror at an object on her bed.

The doll had been crafted to look like Carrie Whiting. Blond hair surrounded a beautiful face, and the dress was elegant. The doll would have made an excellent gift for a little girl except for the large knife which had been plunged into its heart.

Carrie pressed a hand against her forehead and closed her eyes. When she opened them again she appeared composed. "I'm sorry . . . when I came inside and saw that . . ."

"You have nothing to apologize for." Dehner took a few quick steps toward the woman and place a hand on each shoulder. "Are you all right?"

"Yes, I'm fine."

The detective checked the room's one window, which was locked and showed no sign of being tampered with. He then returned to the room's door. "Miss Whiting, did you lock this door and the window when you last left the room?"

"Of course," came the immediate reply. "I long ago got in the habit of locking up when I'm gone. You'd be surprised at some of the crazy stunts fans can pull, not to mention newspaper reporters."

"There's no sign that someone broke in."

Pounding footsteps sounded on the stairway. Rance stepped out of the room as a wiry man wearing thick glasses and a vest with two buttons missing came running down the hall. Dehner recognized the man as Eliab Purvis, the desk clerk and probably more.

"Do you own this hotel, Mr. Purvis?"

The man stopped at the open doorway and looked about as if confused by the question. "Sure do, I sold my ranch two years ago and—"

"Miss Whiting has one key to this room. Are there any duplicates?"

"Yep, a hotel owner needs—"

"Where are the duplicates kept?" Dehner asked.

"On a rack under the main desk downstairs."

"How many people know about the duplicates?"

Purvis looked even more confused as he shrugged his shoulders. "Can't say, I haven't tried to keep it a secret."

"And you leave the main desk unattended frequently, don't you, Mr. Purvis?"

"What choice have I got, there is—"

"I'll need the duplicate key to Miss Whiting's room."

A knowing smile appeared on Purvis's face. Dehner's glare vanquished it.

The hotel owner now seemed anxious to please. He opened the palm of his right hand. "I have it right here! I figured the scream came from Miss Whiting's room, so naturally I brought the key."

"Naturally," Dehner took the key from the hotel owner.

A smiling Carrie Whiting joined the two men. She assured Eliab Purvis there was nothing to worry about and laughed about her scream. "Sometimes I get scared by my own shadow. I hope I didn't disturb the other guests."

Eliab went on at length about how the Songbird of the West was a joy to have at the Purvis Hotel. Both Carrie and Rance were relieved when Purvis returned to his desk. They slowly walked back to the doll which was still sitting upright on the bed, propped against a pillow.

"So, you don't want Mr. Purvis to know what really made you scream."

Carrie glanced back toward the door, making sure it was closed. "What's the point?"

Dehner picked up the doll. "This toy looks like you, what—"

"It's a Carrie Whiting Doll," Carrie stood directly beside the detective. "George McLeod sold the rights to produce those dolls to a toy company . . . oh . . . about sixteen months ago."

"When did they come out?" The detective asked.

"Let me think . . . it's September now . . . probably about a year ago. I know they sold very well last Christmas."

"Speaking of George McLeod, do you know where he is?" Dehner pointed to the left with his thumb. "He is obviously not in his room."

"Before my concert this afternoon, George told me he was having dinner with the mayor and his wife. George didn't want to do it but the mayor pretty much insisted and George likes to keep people happy. I promised him I'd stay close to you."

Rance noted that Carrie's hands trembled a bit. The singer was still shaken but she was getting her emotions under control, or appeared to be.

"I'll be talking with his honor myself, first thing in the morning."

"Why?"

The detective nodded at the doll in his hands. "This thing is new. I met Mayor Felix Murphy earlier today and he bragged about owning the town's only mercantile. I can't think of any other store in town where a toy like this could be purchased. . . ."

Dehner droned on for a few minutes about questioning Murphy in regard to people who had purchased Carrie Whiting dolls. Carrie gave no response and there was a nervous silence.

"If you don't mind Miss Whiting, I'll keep this doll."

"Please do. I never want to see it again."

"Well Miss Whiting, there doesn't seem—"

"Please, call me Carrie."

"Thank you, Miss, ah, Carrie, it would bring me great pleasure to do that. And, of course, you can call me Rance."

"What was her name, Rance?"

"Whose name?"

"At supper, I kidded you about rescuing damsels in distress. For a moment, your face went ashen. There was a very important lady in your life. Someone you couldn't save."

A shock passed through Dehner's body. He began to feel a sense of intimacy with Carrie Whiting. This was a woman who had trusted him with a story of her life that could, if used in the wrong way, destroy her career. Maybe she would understand the demon clawing at his soul. "I could have saved her, but failed because of my own pride. Her name was Beth Page."

Speaking that name out loud rattled the detective. He avoided his companion's eyes.

"What happened, Rance?"

"I was a deputy sheriff in a small town, sort of like this one. I was sixteen. Beth was fourteen. We fell in love the way only people that age can do."

"Go on."

"Beth was in the sheriff's office with me one day. She was talking about a new dress she was making for a dance coming up that Saturday night. Someone barged in with news about trouble in a saloon. The sheriff was out of town. I went to see about it."

"It must have been serious."

Dehner nodded his head. "The moment I stepped into the saloon, I knew there was going to be gunplay. Out of the corner of my eye, I could see Beth. She was standing on the boardwalk outside the saloon, looking over the batwings."

"She followed you there. Not surprising, she loved—"

Dehner interrupted with a shout. "I should have left the saloon right then and taken her home. But my damned pride! I didn't want to be mocked by a bunch of gunneys."

The detective went silent. His breathing was heavy and quick.

Carrie placed a hand on his arm. "You were sixteen and afraid of looking like a coward. That's no reason to be ashamed."

Dehner's voice was now a whisper. "When the gunfire started, I dropped to the floor for protection. Beth thought I had been shot. She ran inside to get to me and was hit by a stray bullet."

"Oh, no . . ."

"She died within minutes."

"Rance, it wasn't your fault."

"Yes it was. And I need to live a life of what the preachers call repentance, to never again be a man who places his own pride above the needs of others."

Dehner paused, feeling vulnerable and exposed as well as embarrassed by his confession. An artificial smile cut across his face as his voice became buoyant. "Besides, you were right, being a detective is like being a singer, there are a lot of fine rewards."

The two stared at each other, both feeling that one significant word or gesture could forever change both of their lives. But neither seemed capable of that word or gesture.

When Rance spoke there was sadness in his voice as if something irretrievable had just been surrendered. "Well, for the second time, I'll wish you good night, Carrie."

The woman followed Dehner to the door. Not until he was outside the room and she stood in the doorway did Carrie reply, "Good night, Rance."

As Dehner prepared for bed he could hear Carrie singing a love song. The words seemed to ooze through the wall in a seductive manner. Was the song for him? Did Carrie Whiting want him to—

Dehner cursed himself silently for his foolish notions. Singing was Carrie's life. She probably sang to herself every night as she got ready for bed.

Rance Dehner had trouble falling asleep. When sleep did come it brought a cascade of vivid dreams. But when the detective awoke, he could remember none of them. The dreams had been wiped from his consciousness.

"Just as well," Dehner said out loud to an empty room.

Chapter Eleven

George McLeod stood on the porch of the Murphy home and lied about having had a wonderful evening. He was happy to be done with it. This visit had dragged on far too long.

Mayor Felix Murphy was playfully shaking a fist in McLeod's direction. "I read about all your fights in the papers. You know, I did some amateur boxing myself."

"Amateur says it all!" his wife, Andrea, cut in. "He use ta git himself beat up in the schoolyard every day."

Andrea Murphy was a woman of less than average height, overweight by a few pounds. Like her husband, she was past thirty but still a long ride from forty.

McLeod exchanged some more jocular remarks with the couple and then departed. His mind mused over the fact that this visit had been a matter of habit, not necessity. Carrie's career was far past the point where he had to butter up small town officials in hopes of getting his client another engagement in their backwater.

The Murphys' house was at the northern edge of the town. The agent walked cautiously through the darkness of the night. The stars and moon were still playing hooky from Dry River. He could see the town's main street and a broken line of filmy yellow blotches coming from the hotel and saloons. The lanterns which hung over most of the stores were now out.

Hard to believe that next week, we'll be heading for New York, George mused silently. He was still relishing that thought when something hard pressed into his back.

"Be quiet and do what I say!" The order came from a low guttural voice.

"What the—"

"Put your hands up and walk left . . . under the tree."

McLeod did what he was told. Darkness now enveloped him even more than before. "My wallet is in my coat pocket."

"I ain't no petty thief, Mr. McLeod. I'm a lot more ambitious."

"What do you mean?"

"I'm sure you remember where the Kimball ranch is located."

"The place those kidnappers took Carrie—"

"Yep, Mr. McLeod, the ranch is deserted now. But tomorra night at midnight you're gonna be there with three thousand dollars."

"What the hell!"

The gunman pressed his weapon harder into George's back. "Do it, or something awful will happen to Miss Whiting."

"You can't get close to Carrie! She's being guarded—"

"Oh, I've already proved you wrong about that."

McLeod's voice rose in alarm. "What've you done?"

"I don't think Miss Whiting is going to sleep well tonight. You see, when she got back to her room there was a surprise waiting for her: a Carrie Whiting doll with a knife through it."

"You bastard!"

"Now, now, Mr. McLeod, there's nothing to worry about. A knife through a doll won't hurt anyone. Now, a knife through Miss Whiting—"

"I'll need more time. I can't raise that much money in one day!"

"Yes, you can! Everyone knows you're Carrie Whiting's manager. Why, that's better than managing a gold mine. Talk to Chet Bellamy at the bank. He'll loan you three thousand."

Heavy footsteps sounded from a distance. They were advancing at a steady pace.

"See you tomorra at midnight, McLeod. Don't be late!" The gunman ran off, creating a barely audible swish against the ground and even that slight sound quickly diminished into nothingness.

"I'm up against someone fast and limber," the former boxer whispered to himself.

Footsteps continued to clomp towards him. A bulge appeared in the darkness. McLeod unbuttoned his coat and moved a hand toward the gun in his shoulder holster.

"Hello." The male voice sounded anxious and vaguely apologetic.

"Hello," George replied as he moved his hand down.

The figure stopped only a few feet from the agent. "I'm Laszlo, remember me?"

"Ah, sure, Laszlo, you're the swamper at the saloon."

"It must be really nice."

"I don't follow you."

"You're Carrie Whiting's boss. She's very pretty. It must be really nice."

McLeod mused briefly on the fact that he had to protect a client whose life had just been threatened. Still, a kind element came into his voice. "Yes, it's really nice."

"My job isn't nice."

"Oh."

"Tonight, some men spills whiskey and Wally the barkeep asks me to clean it up. So, I tries to do my job but those men knocks me over and laughs at me. That's not nice. That's not right!"

"You're right, Laszlo. But why did you come out here?"

"I'm going to tell the mayor! The mayor is nice to me, his wife too. Sometimes I do stuff for them at the store."

Laszlo looked in the direction of the Murphy

home. "I guess it's late, maybe tomorrow."

"Yep, I think waiting for tomorrow is a good idea. Why don't you just walk around for a little while, allow the jaspers who gave you a hard time to leave. Then, go back to the saloon and do your job for the night."

"OK. Can I walk beside you?"

George cringed inwardly but his better nature prevailed. He needed to get back to the hotel, but Carrie was not in immediate danger and Rance Dehner was with her, or at least, in the room next door. He had time for a small act of kindness.

"Sure, Laszlo."

As they began their walk, McLeod attempted a friendly question. "Have you lived in Dry River very long?"

"I'm not sure."

"Oh."

"I use to live in another town. The people there are nice. Most of them. They say I takes part in a big fight with a lot of other men. I even gets to wear a uniform in the fight. But my head gets hurt bad and I don't remember . . . you know."

McLeod suddenly felt angry with himself for not wanting to give this man a few minutes of his time. "Yes, I'm pretty sure I know. Why did you leave that town, Laszlo?"

"The stage line gets a new coach that's very pretty. I want to ride on it. So, I save my money from working at the stable and one day buy a ticket. I ride the stage and it stops at a lot of towns. But when it gets to Dry River the driver say I have to pay more money or gets off. I already give them all my money."

"So, you just stayed in Dry River?"

Laszlo nodded his head. "Some people asks me where I come from but I can't remembers. I gets a job at the saloon, and works some for Murphy's Mercantile, and sometimes the hotel, but only when it's busy."

They stopped in front of the Hotel. George's eyes went immediately to the second floor which was completely dark. Carrie must have found the doll, shown it to Dehner and was now trying to get some sleep.

"She's very pretty."

McLeod's attention snapped back to his companion. "Excuse me?"

"Carrie Whiting, she's very pretty."

"Yes." The agent looked down the street toward the saloon. "Things seem to have quieted down at the Silver Crown. I think it's OK for you to go back now. Nice talking to you!"

George walked briskly into the hotel. Laszlo stood alone in the darkness staring toward the second floor of the hotel.

"She's very pretty," he said.

Chapter Twelve

The sky was red streaked as Dehner made his way to the sheriff's office. He was joined on the boardwalk by Curt Weldon.

"Good morning, Mr. Detective!"

"Good morning, Mr. Deputy. You seem cheerful this morning."

"Yep, had a good night's sleep. Last night was the sheriff's turn to sleep on the job. I'll tell yuh, that old cot in the office gives a man a sore back, and hearing a bunch of drunks snoring sure don't make for a restful night. But Sheriff Streeter don't mind much. He may be sawing logs when we march in."

The two men stopped at the office and Weldon slipped a key into the door, only to find it already unlocked. "Whatcha got in that old potato sack?"

"Something pretty ugly," Dehner said as the two men stepped inside.

Weldon's speculation had been wrong. Sheriff Tal Streeter was awake and sitting at his desk, sipping coffee and looking over flyers. Irritation blanketed his face when he saw Dehner arrive with Curt. The lawman knew the detective was bringing more trouble.

"Mornin' gents," he pointed toward a coffee

pot perched atop a small stove. "Help yourselves. But Curt, you better drink your java real quick."

"Whaddya mean?"

"Ezra Brown sent one of his hands into town to get me outta bed this mornin'. Ezra woke up with the chickens a few hours ago. Looked outside and thought he saw a stranger sneakin' around. It was dark, o' course. He stepped out onto his porch and the stranger started shootin' at him."

"Why?" Curt asked.

The sheriff threw up his hands. "Ezra don't know! He ducked back into his house and grabbed a rifle. When he looked out his window the shooter was gone."

"What was the name of the ranch hand you talked with?" Curt spoke in a calm manner. His boss was obviously in a bad mood.

"Larry . . . somethin' . . . I can't remember." Streeter took another sip of coffee and gave his two companions a wan smile as if apologizing for his grouchiness, then settled his glance on Curt. "Ezra Brown is a man who likes to handle things hisself. If he's sendin' for the law, well, I think there might be somethin' more to this. I want you to ride out there and jaw with him and some of the hands, see what you can find out."

"Sure."

The sheriff took another sip of coffee and his eyes became playful. He understood the lack of enthusiasm in his deputy's response.

"Ezra's ranch ain't that far out. Leave right now, thataway you'll be back in plenty of time to hear Carrie Whiting sing tonight."

Second time around, Curt Weldon's "Sure" was spoken with a lot more zeal. He hurried from the office.

Dehner poured himself some coffee as he watched Curt's fast exit. Tal pointed to the sack Rance had placed on his desk. "Whatever you got in there, I figure it ain't good news."

The detective nodded his head and pulled out the Carrie Whiting doll with a knife in its heart. While consuming his coffee, Dehner explained about the doll and the situation with the keys at the hotel.

"You're right," the lawman replied to Dehner's account. "Murphy's Mercantile is the only place in town that would sell a doll like this one. Felix and Andrea open early; let's get over there and wish 'em a good morning."

"Why, good morning to you, Tal! Mister, I know yuh and me got introduced yesterday but I can't remember yore name. But, say, ain't yuh a detective?"

Rance Dehner gave the woman his name and confirmed his occupation.

The counter of Murphy's Mercantile ran parallel to a side wall of shelves and almost reached a back wall. Andrea Murphy stood behind it. She had a wide face and a smile that fit it well.

"Where's Curt?" she asked.

"I sent him off to do a job," Streeter replied.

The woman laughed in a hearty manner, as if the sheriff had just told a joke. "Poor boy! Most times, he has breakfast at Peterson's restaurant, then after he eats his chuck, he comes in here to buy a piece of rock candy; likes to suck on it while he does his rounds."

Felix Murphy entered from a back room. He was carrying a carton of canned goods. "Howdy gents!" Murphy's greeting was friendly but had an edge. He knew the two newcomers hadn't arrived to buy rock candy or anything else.

"Can you folks give us a few moments?" Streeter asked. "This shouldn't take long."

"What kinda mayor wouldn't give the town's sheriff the time of day?" Andrea turned to her husband. "Put yore burden down and git over here."

Felix did as his wife instructed. He placed his hands on the counter and gave a mechanical smile, "What can I do for you?"

Tal Streeter pointed to the three Carrie Whiting dolls that perched on the store's top shelf. "How many of those do yuh have in stock?"

"We ordered two dozen," Felix answered.

"Thanks to me!" His wife proclaimed.

Dehner was beginning to understand which of the Murphys was the most informative. "What do you mean, Mrs. Murphy?"

"Felix only wanted to order us a half dozen of those dolls, seeing how they cost so much. He said most folks in Dry River couldn't afford it. I reminded his honor that folks would be coming from all over to see Carrie Whiting and not all those folks would be poor. Why, that young lady ain't quite twenty yet and she's the talk of the whole world. I only made me one mistake."

Dehner smiled benignly, "What was that?"

"Shoulda ordered more! Them three dolls yuh see on the shelf is all we got left!"

Tal returned the questioning to Felix. "Can you remember at least some of the people who bought the twenty-one dolls?"

The mayor laughed harshly and shook his head. "Most of the time, Andrea or I could tell you the names of every customer we had the previous week. But with all the strangers we got in town now . . . having Carrie Whiting in Dry River has changed everything."

Andrea grinned at her husband's remark. "Tal, that deputy of yores was eying those dolls yesterday. Tole me he'd rob a bank and give me all the loot he had if I could sell him the real Carrie Whiting to take home. Yuh know, I think he was half-serious."

• • •

The trail to Ezra Brown's ranch was a familiar one and Curt Weldon was allowing his imagination free rein. He and Carrie Whiting had just completed their honeymoon and returned to Dry River where . . .

Reality began to infect Curt's daydream. Why would Carrie Whiting settle for living in Dry River? After all, the Songbird of the West was in demand in cities like Denver, New York and . . .

Reality's harsh arrow continued to bore in. Carrie Whiting made more money than he did! Why, she earned a lot more money than most men! What would it really be like to be her husband? The man who married the Songbird of the West would have to travel around with her and fume while other men watched his wife sing and dance. Did he really want to live like that?

Weldon never got to answer his own question. A sharp pain cut into his shoulder an instant after he heard a shot. He folded onto his horse's neck and tried to hold on. A second shot missed but panicked the black that neighed loudly as it lifted onto its hind legs, dropped Curt to the ground and bolted.

Curt struggled to his feet. He was in a life or death fight and knew it. The deputy thought he heard a rifle leveraging from the top of a hill he was facing. Weldon now only had the use of one arm. The lawman pulled his .45 and fired in the direction of the sound. His action got a quick response. He saw a figure appear from behind a boulder on the hill. Looking at the assailant, Curt was also looking directly into the bright sun. An array of black dots danced around the man with a rifle as he flamed another shot, this one scorching into the deputy's chest.

Weldon once again hit the ground. This time he knew he couldn't get up. His only hope was to play dead.

The hot pain that gripped his body made lying still hard but he managed it. He remained immobile for several minutes after hearing the thud of hooves running down the hill and into the distance. Then, unable to contain the hurt anymore, he doubled up and began to cry.

"Bawling like a damn baby ain't gonna help you none." The deputy managed to sit up. Squinting his eyes against a merciless sun, he saw an occasional shadow flicker on the trail ahead and heard a soft nickering sound.

His black hadn't run off very far. The animal was grazing at the side of the hill. "You gotta get to that horse, Weldon, your life depends on it."

The deputy's whispered words provided the encouragement to get onto his feet, but the process was painful and slow. Standing, the lawman had to battle nausea and struggle to keep his consciousness.

Curt left a trail of blood behind him as he

staggered toward his horse. When he reached the animal he drank from his canteen which was less than a quarter full. The deputy hadn't thought it necessary to check the canteen before leaving on such a short ride.

The lawman leaned on his horse and tried to quell the panic building inside him. "The grim reaper's got a hold on you, Weldon, but just maybe you can break loose."

Again, Curt's whispered words brought him encouragement. He carefully thought over his dilemma. He was about half way between town and Ezra Brown's ranch. He didn't have the stamina for the ride back or forward. But he reckoned he could make it to nearby Stony Creek. There he could have plenty of water to bathe his wounds and drink as much as he could to replace the blood he was losing.

Nausea continued to cripple Weldon's resolve. He wanted to lie down in the grass and sleep. But he knew the rest would be surrendering to death. He inhaled deeply and then mounted the black.

On top of the steed, Curt slumped forward and again embraced the horse's neck. The black, which had just finished grazing, needed only the slightest prod to head for the creek.

When they arrived at the water, the lawman succeeded in slipping off his horse without collapsing. As he drank from the creek, Weldon began to feel optimistic about his chances for survival. *Ezra Brown and his ranch hands will be wanting to see Carrie Whiting tonight. They'll be riding into town. At least some of them will stop here to refresh their horses. They'll find me and take me into town.*

"I'll have to rest a spell in Doc Harding's office," Curt said aloud. "Doc's really excited about seeing Carrie Whiting again, I'll have to wait . . ."

The notion impressed Curt Weldon as being funny. He began to laugh uncontrollably and then the world went dark.

The deputy awoke to searing pain. Nausea overwhelmed him and he realized he couldn't even sit up. He looked at the sun to see how long he had been out. Two to three hours, he reckoned.

The optimism he had experienced before was gone. He doubted if he could hang on until Ezra and his boys arrived.

Footsteps sounded from nearby. Hope again surged through the young lawman. "Over here," his voice was weak but loud enough.

"Hello Curt."

Weldon smiled at the familiar face that looked down at him. "Sure am happy to see yuh. . . ."

The deputy's smile vanished as he looked into the cold eyes that now peered over a gun barrel. The new pain that seared into him was brief as the grim reaper took his final slash.

Chapter Thirteen

Dehner sat at Sheriff Tal Streeter's desk and worried. Early that morning, George McLeod had told him about the gunman who stopped him near the Murphys' home. But McLeod had insisted Dehner keep mum and not tell the law. The detective complied but didn't like it.

Rance's mind began to wrestle with the question of the gunman's identity. He had one theory which seemed to—

An angry Tal Streeter barged into the office. "I appreciate yuh holding the fort for me, Rance."

"You did take a bit longer than I expected." Dehner's reply was good natured.

Streeter's eyes went to the ceiling. "I just wasted me a whole ton of time lookin' for a stolen horse that wasn't really stolen. The guy's brother had borrowed it!"

Dehner made a lopsided grin. "All part of a lawdog's job. You can't apprehend vicious outlaws every day."

"Suppose you're right but . . ."

Hoof beats slowed to a stop outside of the sheriff's office. Streeter turned and looked out the window. "That's Ezra Brown and his boys, guess they came into town early to do some hoorawin' before Carrie Whiting sings."

"I wonder if Curt is—"

The sheriff suddenly bolted from the office. Dehner followed him. When the detective got outside he saw seven horsemen: six of them were young. The older man was white haired, his skin a mass of wrinkles from a life spent in the sun.

Streeter looked at the older man. "Hello, Ezra."

"Hello, Tal." Ezra Brown spoke as he dismounted.

Both men spoke in a grim voice. One of Brown's ranch hands was holding the reins of a horse which had a body lying across it. Brown grabbed the reins of the riderless horse and brought it forward.

The rancher tilted his head at the body which was wrapped in an old tarp. "It's Curt Weldon. We found him by Stony Creek. He'd been shot three times. I'm sorry."

Brown's sorrow seemed genuine but tempered by many years of a hard life. In the West, death was a frequent occurrence and often brought down the young.

Tal started toward the body. Brown held up a palm. "Don't look at him here, Tal. The last shot he took was at close range. He's bloody. We had to wrap him real careful."

The sheriff pressed thin lips together and nodded his head.

Dehner sensed that Tal Streeter couldn't talk without his voice breaking. The detective felt grief and shock over the murder of Curt Weldon. But he hadn't known Weldon as long as the sheriff.

Rance wanted to give Tal a chance to collect himself. He hastily explained who he was to Ezra Brown and his men. "Curt was riding out to your ranch, Mr. Brown. The sheriff wanted him to look into that shooting this morning."

"Shooting? Whatcha talking about?"

"Didn't someone take a shot at you, very early this morning?"

"No. If anyone had, I'da gone after the snake myself."

Dehner continued, "So, you didn't send one of your hands into town to tell the sheriff someone tried to shoot you?"

"Hell, no." The rancher's eyes did a quick scan of his six men, all of whom were still mounted. "Any of yus know what this man's talking about?" His question was met with shrugs and shaking heads.

All eyes shifted to Tal Streeter. The sheriff had no more time to compose himself. Dehner spoke softly. "Tal, you said earlier that the ranch hand's name was Larry. Can you tell us any more about him?"

"Like I said before, he woke me up. I remember him wearin' a new red checkered shirt, and a white Stetson that also looked new. There wasn't a spot of dirt on the shirt or the hat. That's about all I remember about him."

Ezra Brown pushed back his own dusty Stetson and scratched his head. "Didn't yuh think that sorta strange?"

"Yep, but ranch hands are strange when it comes to spendin' money, especially if they get an eye on some gal."

Brown sighed deeply, "Guess yuh gotta point."

"Whoever came to the office this morning was smart or was working for someone who was smart," Dehner said.

"I don't follow yuh," Brown replied.

"The man wore a new shirt and hat to distract the sheriff, who was just waking up. Now we have no description of the man who called himself Larry."

Curious onlookers were collecting across the street. The sheriff's voice was a low, angry rumble. "Guess we'd better get him to Doc Harding."

"I'm afraid it's too late for a doctor," Dehner said. "We need an undertaker."

"Yuh don't know this here town very good Mr. Dehner." Brown mounted his piebald. "Doc Harding is also the undertaker."

Chapter Fourteen

Dehner glanced out the window of Carrie Whiting's room. A sense of excitement filled the town's main street. None of the stirring related to the murder of Deputy Curt Weldon. The Songbird of the West would be performing at the Silver Crown in less than an hour.

Rance turned and faced the singer, who was dabbing at her eyes with a handkerchief. George McLeod was standing beside his client with one hand perched delicately on her shoulder. The room contained one chair but it remained empty.

"I'm sorry to tell you this before a performance Carrie, but I thought it dangerous for you not to know."

"It's OK, Rance, I feel so sorry about Curt Weldon. He was one of the men who rescued me from those kidnappers and he seemed such a fine person. . . ."

George McLeod's eyes had widened a bit when he heard the detective and his client calling each other by their first names. McLeod would probably ask Carrie about the situation later in the evening. Dehner wondered what she would tell him.

For that matter, he wondered what there was

to tell. On the previous night there had been a sudden and intense feeling of intimacy between Carrie Whiting and the man hired to protect her. That intimacy was gone now . . . replaced by what?

Dehner inhaled and shook such thoughts from his mind. Carrie could be in real danger and it was his job to make sure nothing happened to her.

"I accompanied Tal Streeter when he took Curt's body to Doc Harding," Dehner continued. "The deputy had been shot three times: twice with a rifle and once up close with a pistol."

"He must have been shot long range with the rifle," McLeod said. "Then, the snake checked to make sure the poor kid was dead. When he saw Weldon still breathing, the killer drew his pistol and finished the job."

"Maybe," Dehner replied. "The doctor removed Curt's clothes. I looked through them and found this in his shirt pocket."

Dehner handed McLeod a small piece of paper which had been ripped from a larger sheet and folded four times. George took his hand off Carrie's shoulder as he unfolded the paper. Both the singer and her agent read the words scrawled large in a child-like manner: THIS TIME NO DEPUTY TO SAVE ANGEL.

George McLeod whispered a curse. The singer closed her eyes and said nothing.

Dehner kept his voice low. "Carrie, you have told George and me about Skeet being beaten up by a deputy sheriff when he tried to take you from the home of Reverend Barton. Have you told anybody else?"

"No."

"Do you have any notion as to whether Skeet has told anyone?"

"He says he's kept silent on the matter. I believe him."

McLeod added: "Besides, why would Jones tell anyone about being pounded by a lawman while trying to kidnap Carrie? Say, did you show that note to the sheriff or the doc?"

"No. They were both busy examining Curt's wounds. I knew you wouldn't want me to say anything about this to anyone. But I think it's a bad idea keeping Streeter in the dark."

The agent ignored Dehner's last statement. "So, it has to be Skeet Jones who killed the deputy and left the note in his pocket . . . a note he knew only we would understand."

"I don't believe Skeet could kill anyone, except in self defense," Carrie said.

Dehner tugged at his right ear. "Whoever did it didn't necessarily do the killing himself."

The singer looked confused. "What do you mean?"

"I think there's a hired killer in the mix."

"How do you figure that?" McLeod asked.

"The night we pried Carrie loose from that gang of thugs, one of them escaped. At first I thought he just ran off, but he might have circled around and returned to town to report what happened to whoever was paying him. With a crowd of people in Dry River to hear Carrie, it would be easy for a stranger to blend in."

"But you spotted him in your field glasses while—"

Dehner grimaced and shook his head as he interrupted the agent. "I didn't get all that good a look at him. I wouldn't recognize his face."

"And you think Skeet Jones still has this jasper on his payroll?" McLeod asked.

"Skeet seems our best choice. But why did he write that note I found? It points directly to him!"

"What should we do, Rance?"

Carrie's voice indicated complete trust in Dehner's abilities. The detective hoped the trust wasn't misplaced. "Well, since you two are both in show business, you could say that tonight I'm going to be a stand in for George. I'm going to make that trip out to the Kimball ranch."

"No, Dehner, I can handle this myself," McLeod snapped. "I borrowed the three thousand from the bank a few hours ago."

Rance snapped back. "Return the money first thing in the morning. That'll keep your interest payments low. I'm going to meet this jasper tonight with a saddle bag filled with ripped paper.

My idea is not to pay extortion but to learn more about what is going on."

"That sounds very dangerous, Rance."

The detective smiled whimsically. "Yes, Carrie, it is dangerous. But I'm hired to do dangerous things." Dehner shifted his eyes to McLeod. "George, you have a very important job ahead. You're managing the career of Carrie Whiting, the Songbird of the West. Don't let anything get in the way of that."

McLeod lifted his cigar toward Dehner as if making a toast. "We'll do it your way, for tonight at least. Right now, we have to get over to the Silver Crown."

The two men accompanied Carrie as she made her way down the stairs. When they reached the lobby George and Rance walked on each side of the singer as she hastily walked toward the back door, pretending not to see the few people in the lobby who were gawking at her. The Songbird of the West was to start her show within fifteen minutes. There was no time to give fans individual attention.

Outside, the threesome picked up their pace as they made their way past the backsides of several buildings to reach the saloon. Dehner made several glances behind him; no one was following. Good.

The back door of the Silver Crown stood open. Skeet Jones filled the doorway but immediately stepped sideways to make way for his major attraction.

"The house is packed!" Something strange inflamed Jones's eyes but Rance couldn't tell what it was. "This is going to be a big night!"

"Yes," Dehner replied. "I'm sure it's going to be a big night."

Chapter Fifteen

Dehner and George McLeod both stood beside the small platform in the Silver Crown. Behind them a pianist was doing a passable rendition of *The Merry, Merry Month of May* as part of the fifteen minute prelude that came before Carrie Whiting's performance.

"Jones promised us a decent pianist to accompany Carrie," McLeod's voice was angry and low. "I was a fool to believe him."

Dehner reckoned McLeod's anger was really aimed at the customers that packed the saloon. Many were already well on the path to becoming drunk. Lewd remarks about mating with a songbird accompanied boisterous guffaws.

As if to prove the detective right, McLeod looked angrily over the room. "Carrie's days of singing in rat holes like this ended over two years ago. She shouldn't be doing this now, may Skeet Jones be damned!"

The pianist pounded the keys harder as he began to play *Swanee River*, the song which preceded Carrie's entrance. George McLeod tilted his head towards Dehner's ear before speaking again. "You stand near the side wall where you can stop anyone who tries to rush the stage. I'll be in the back, looking for any trouble."

Dehner nodded and walked toward the far left side of the Silver Crown while McLeod positioned himself near the batwings. The saloon was packed. All the tables were filled and lines of men formed a wide horseshoe around the room.

The pianist finished with *Swanee River* and Felix Murphy ran onto the stage. "Men, I know you're not here tonight to see me!" He gave a loud laugh and continued. "So I will get right down to business. Mr. Skeet Jones is proud to have brought the Songbird of the West to Dry River . . . and so . . . for the second of her three performances here in our fine town, I give you Miss Carrie Whiting!"

Carrie stepped out from the door to the right of the bar. Loud applause and raucous shouts followed her as she made her way onto the stage. Dehner noted that with her entrance, the lewd remarks ceased. Carrie Whiting had that kind of impact on people.

The singer beamed a smile at the audience. "Thank you, Mr. Mayor; thanks to everyone for coming. I hope you enjoy the show."

An alcohol laced voice yelled from a back table. "After the show, I'd sure enjoy a little stroll with you, sweetie."

Carrie's smile didn't waver. "Sorry sir, but

I only take strolls with men who can walk straight!"

Laughter blared across the Silver Crown and Dehner noted the professional demeanor of the Songbird of the West. Maybe she was over two years past singing in rat holes, as George McLeod put it, but she had obviously learned much from the experience.

Carrie motioned with one hand toward the pianist. "Stanley and I would like to get things off to a lively start . . ."

Carrie's performance totally captivated her audience. Men were enthusiastically clapping and whistling as Carrie sang *Camp Town Races*.

Rance Dehner's attention remained on his job. He noticed the door to the right of the bar opening once again. The detective tensed as he didn't see anyone step through the door. Whoever came in was bent low in order to be shielded by the bar. But of course, the customers standing at the far right in the Silver Crown could spot the intruder. He would have to strike fast.

Dehner ran toward the stage as a ghostly figure emerged from the side of the bar and charged toward Carrie. A loud screech coursed over the saloon as the wearer of a white sheet lifted his hands and thrust them in the direction of the singer.

Rance tackled the intruder just before he reached the platform. The white sheet billowed up and momentarily embraced Dehner as the detective and the ghost slammed against the floor. The music stopped.

Dehner buoyed up and lifted the sheet. "Laszlo, what are—"

"I only joke. Miss Carrie likes jokes—"

Laszlo's pleas were cut off by a large, overweight man who rose from his front table with surprising speed. "Yuh stupid idiot, I'm gonna—"

"Leave him alone!" The songbird's voice snapped with authority. Suddenly the room was silent and Carrie realized she had just humiliated a man who likely had to endure plenty of taunts about his weight. She needed to calm the situation.

The smile returned to her face. "I appreciate your help. I know things looked scary but it was only a joke. Please sit down." The man did as he was asked.

Carrie sent a quick glance over the audience. "How many of you were here yesterday for the matinee?" There was a large showing of hands.

The singer continued. "Well, Laszlo did a lot of work to make sure that the matinee could happen. He stacked tables and lined up the chairs, so the families of this town could enjoy the show. For all his hard work, I promised him he could play a joke on me tonight."

The singer motioned toward Laszlo who was now standing in front of the platform beside Dehner. "Let's have some applause for a hard working man who knows how to pull a knee slapper!"

As applause filled the saloon, Carrie walked over to the two men in front of her. That enchanting smile remained on her face as she spoke in a quick whisper. Most people in the audience probably thought the singer was talking to Laszlo. In fact, she was whispering to Dehner. "Keep an eye on him, Rance. Don't let anyone hurt him."

With Laszlo at his side, Dehner returned to his place at the far left of the Silver Crown. He made a quick glance toward George McLeod who nodded at him approvingly.

A satisfied client always makes a detective happy, Rance mused silently. But he was even happier about the way Carrie had handled a potentially explosive situation. If that rotund gent had tried to hurt Laszlo, Dehner would have had to stop him and a fight would have followed. With a room full of rowdy men, many of them boozed up, there could have been a riot.

And Carrie had been right about needing to protect Laszlo. Dehner noticed several hostile eyes on the swamper as he walked beside him. The saloon patrons knew the story about a joke was a polite fantasy. But the swamper's antics were forgotten for the moment as eyes returned to the show.

No one was more entranced by the singer's performance than Laszlo. Dehner realized this was a very special night for the swamper. Laszlo had received a compliment from the Songbird of the West and she had asked a packed house to applaud him.

Dehner again glanced at the man standing beside him. There was wildness in the eyes that fastened on the show. A wildness that incorporated love, enchantment, and . . . There was something else there Dehner couldn't identify. Something dangerous that could lead to calamity.

Chapter Sixteen

Carrie Whiting was throwing a kiss to the audience following her encore when Skeet Jones jumped onto the platform. The saloon owner loudly proclaimed, "Remember gents, tomorrow night will be Carrie's last performance in Dry River. As for right now, well, the Silver Crown is open for business!"

Jones turned to face the singer but she had already departed the stage. George McLeod and Tal Streeter hastily walked her out of the saloon by the same route she had come in.

Dehner sighed and felt pity for Tal Streeter. Curt Weldon's body was lying in a shack behind Doc Harding's office but the sheriff had no time to grieve. Earlier that day the lawman had agreed to help escort Carrie back to the hotel.

"Sure . . . I need to be on duty tonight." Streeter didn't ask why Dehner couldn't help with the escort. As he spoke, the lawman's face looked pale and defeated. Tal Streeter was probably the only man in Dry River who would be happy to see Carrie Whiting leave town.

Laszlo interrupted the detective's thoughts. "I go to the hotel. They are busy and need me. I come back to clean up."

The swamper paused as if not sure if his next words were proper. "Maybe I visit Miss Carrie at the hotel . . ."

"Miss Carrie is very tired, Laszlo. I think you should leave her alone."

Laszlo nodded his head. "She's very pretty."

"Yes." Dehner replied as Laszlo slowly made his way toward the batwings.

Jones hopped off the platform and began to mix with his customers. There was plenty of time for back slapping. A swarm of men converged on the bar and even with two barkeeps working hard, the wait was long.

Dehner had wanted to remain at the Silver Crown in order to keep an eye on Skeet Jones. George McLeod had been right. Jones was the most likely suspect to have written the note which was found in Curt Weldon's pocket.

But Rance also believed what Carrie said about Skeet: "He wouldn't kill anyone, except in self defense."

Dehner took a tobacco pouch and papers from his pocket and began to build a smoke. The detective only used tobacco now and again. But the process of rolling a cigarette could come in handy when he needed to look occupied.

The detective was riding into a treacherous situation later that night. He hoped that by keeping an eye on Skeet Jones he could ride into it better prepared.

But Jones seemed to have similar notions in mind. As the detective put a flame to his handi-work, the saloon keeper's eyes fused with his. "There seems to be a cat and mouse game here," Dehner whispered to himself. "But who is the cat and who is the mouse?"

The batwings slammed inward with a loud screech. Laszlo stumbled back into the Silver Crown and shouted at the man who had just pushed him inside, "You're mean, Link Howell!"

Link Howell was the rotund man whom Carrie Whiting had stopped from attacking Laszlo. Howell was now enjoying a second chance at assaulting the swamper.

"What's got yuh on the prod, Laszlo? Yuh bein' a man who 'preciates a good joke!"

Howell looked at the small group of men who were watching him bully the swamper. "I jus' tole this moron I could arrange him a meetin' with Carrie. Yuh shoulda seen him. He was shakin' like a dog 'bout to get fed. So, I took him to meet up with Carrie. I forgot to mention, my horse's named Carrie."

Howell bellowed loudly. A few of the onlookers chuckled and looked faintly amused.

"Don't bring me back here now. I need to work at the hotel before I mop the Silver Crown."

"Why sure, Laszlo," there was threat in Howell's voice but the swamper didn't understand it. "Why, Link Howell ain't one to keep a hard workin' man from his job. Yuh jus' go right on ahead."

Link took a step back, bowed and gestured elaborately as if clearing a path to the batwings. As Laszlo rushed to leave, Howell tripped him. The swamper's face collided with the floor.

Howell bellowed once again as Laszlo rolled onto his back, caressing his nose. The rotund man looked downward at his victim. "I thought yuh'd enjoy yourself another joke, before goin' to work."

Link shifted his body and moved one leg backwards preparing for a kick. "Here's one more good laugh—"

Dehner broke through the crowd of men who had now gathered around the spectacle. "The joke is over mister, back off!"

Howell paused. Spotting something fierce in the detective's eyes, he took a step backward.

Rance helped Laszlo to his feet. The swamper pulled out a dirty handkerchief and held it over his nose. "I go to work at hotel. Far away from Link Howell. Get water there to stop bleeding."

The detective took a quick sideways glance. A mob still encircled the bar. Getting a glass of water from one of the barkeeps could take a long time. "Good idea, Laszlo."

Laszlo weaved a bit as he slowly made his way out of the Silver Crown. Link Howell yelled,

"Later on we can do us some more jokin', yuh crazy moron!"

A furious rage stormed inside Rance Dehner. Link Howell was a coward in the very worst sense. He was a man who enjoyed beating up on defenseless men. Dehner knew the type. No doubt Howell also enjoyed roughing up women.

Rance Dehner rarely provoked a fight. He decided this case merited an exception. He took a step toward the coward. "From what I hear, your name is Link Howell."

"Yup."

"I think a rat like you needs a different name. How about Stink Howell the yellow belly?"

Howell suddenly found himself surrounded by mocking laughter. He needed to sound tough but not directly challenge the man in front of him. "Yuh don't know what you're talkin' 'bout, mister."

The smile on Dehner's face also conveyed mockery. "Prove it."

"I don't have ta prove nothin'." Howell turned toward the bar. Dehner grabbed the big man's shoulder, yanked him face forward and plowed a fist into his left eye. Laughter again roared from the spectators as they parted, allowing room for Link Howell to plunge onto the floor.

Dehner shouted over the noise of the crowd. "That eye of yours is going to be black and swollen for a long time, Link. It will give folks

123

something to laugh about every time they see you. A great joker like you should be happy about that!"

The laugher surrounding Link Howell got even louder and was now peppered with insults. Howell would have to endure a lot of mockery about his black eye.

"If you bother Laszlo again, Link, I'll close your other eye. That's a promise!"

The coward looked downward as he got to his feet. "Go 'way. This ain't worth two free drinks."

Dehner's rage suddenly turned on himself as he understood what Link was implying. He grabbed Howell by the front of his shirt. "Who promised you free drinks to beat up Laszlo?"

"The owner of this here place, Skeet Jones."

"Did he say why he wanted you to do it?"

"Na. Jus' said yuh'd come along and rawhide me to stop. Didn't say yuh'd make it a fight."

Dehner let go of Howell and began what he knew would be a futile search for Skeet Jones. The saloon owner wasn't in the Silver Crown or, as Rance discovered as he searched the town, anywhere in Dry River.

The detective figured Jones had ridden out to the Kimball ranch to prepare for their get together later that night. Rance returned to the hotel to talk briefly with George McLeod and make sure everything was fine with Carrie Whiting. He then stopped by the sheriff's office to thank the lawman for helping out that night. But Streeter wasn't in his office.

"Just as well," Rance said to himself. "Tal probably would have asked me if I could be a volunteer deputy tonight. I would have said no and lied to him. I hate to lie to a good person."

Dehner checked his pocket watch. "Time to ride," he said.

Chapter Seventeen

Rance Dehner rode at a steady gait toward a meeting of unknown peril. The sky was a bluish black covered by a carpet of ragged, swirling grey clouds constantly colliding with each other as they blocked the moon.

"I can't figure Jones's involvement in this matter," Rance spoke aloud to his horse. "And there's something else eating at me, but it's just a blur, I can't bring it into focus."

Dehner patted the neck of his bay; he didn't want the animal to be spooked by the anxious tone of his voice. They were now riding by a steep drop, about thirty feet or more of hard gravel and a few large boulders. The trail narrowed only slightly. Still, Dehner reckoned the stage coach that passed by here every day required a first rate jehu.

The detective slowed his horse as he approached the knoll that fronted the Kimball ranch. He dismounted, tied his bay to a tree, and pulled two bags off his saddle. Moving up the hill, it occurred to Dehner that this was the same approach he had taken with Sheriff Streeter, Curt Weldon and George McLeod on the night they rescued Carrie. Streeter knew the Kimball ranch and all of the surrounding territory better than Rance and the detective wished Streeter were with him. But the client, George McLeod, had been insistent that Tal Streeter be kept in the dark.

Dehner recalled what Bertram Lowrie, his boss, was fond of saying: "The wishes of the client receive top priority as long as his cheques clear." McLeod's cheques cleared.

Rance lay on top of the hill and surveyed the scene below. The Kimballs were dead but their ranch had not changed much since he had seen it a little more than twenty-four hours before. There was a ranch house which faced a barn. The corral beside the house now stood empty.

The house would be the best place for the extortionist to hide. He could watch from the window and have protection in the event of a gunfight. Still, the house was an obvious choice and Skeet Jones or whoever it was might possess a fertile imagination. He could be hiding outside somewhere or maybe in the barn.

Dehner slowly advanced down the knoll, remembering that the barn had wide double doors on both the front and back. He flattened himself against the back of the barn and stepped toward the division in the double doors. If someone was hiding inside the barn, he would need a lantern and the light would be visible between the doors.

A horse whinnied from somewhere nearby.

Dehner froze. A shadow emerged from the far side of the barn. The detective dropped to the ground as a bullet keened over him. A loud frightened neigh came from the horse as footsteps ran quickly away.

Dehner buoyed up, drew his .45 and scrambled to the side of the barn where a horse was tied. The chestnut was now trying to break loose, pulling against the reins which were held firm by a hook on the barn wall.

The detective remained close to the barn where extra darkness provided by the overhang made him almost invisible. He listened as the running footsteps hit wood and then went silent.

Something rubbed against Dehner's leg. Rance looked down as a small animal looked up at him and meowed. The cat had probably belonged to the Kimballs. In all likelihood, the feline had been responsible for ridding the place of rodents. Dehner hoped the cat could survive without its masters. Survival in the west was never easy.

A light suddenly appeared in the front window of the ranch house. That made sense . . . sort of. Those footsteps Dehner had listened to had banged on the wooden porch of the ranch house. His adversary made it inside the house where he had lit a lantern.

A nervous nicker came from behind the detective and Dehner realized he was being toyed with by a smart enemy. The adversary had been hiding at the side of the barn with a skittish horse to signal him if someone came near.

But he hadn't slowed his steps when he reached the house's porch. Those steps had become explosions in the quiet of the night. And now the extortionist had a lantern burning as if signaling his location. *He wants me to charge after him and become an easy target,* Dehner thought.

The cat meowed again. Dehner remained still and silent, forcing his enemy to make the next move.

Less than ten minutes had passed when a shout came from the house. "You're not George McLeod."

Dehner shouted back a lie. "Yes, but I've brought three thousand dollars with me."

"Why were you sneaking around behind the barn?"

Did the voice belong to Skeet Jones? Dehner couldn't be sure. His next shout avoided the question. "My gun wasn't drawn. You're the one who fired the first shot."

"Bring the money to the house. Walk slow. Hands high."

Dehner picked up the saddle bags from the ground where he had dropped them. The cat was gone. The shouts had probably rattled the animal which was now hiding somewhere. "Smart guy," Dehner whispered.

Following orders Rance slowly approached

the house. His eyes fastened on the window. He suddenly froze. The lantern's light had reflected off something.

Dehner dived sideways as a shot flashed through the darkness. The detective yanked out his Colt and returned fire.

Rance did a fast sideways crawl. His shot had telegraphed his location. There was only flat ground between the detective and the ranch house: nothing to shield him from a bullet.

A second red-orange spear flamed from the front window of the house. Dehner's Colt again barked a fast response. A silence followed.

Rance lay still, listening carefully for any intrusions into the normal sounds of the night. He didn't have to listen very long. The hoof beats were distant and slow as if someone were walking his horse to avoid being discovered. There was a soft whinny, followed by the thudding of hooves: whoever it was had mounted and ridden off.

Of course, it could all be a trick to make the detective an easy target but Dehner didn't think so. Still, he moved cautiously, in a jackknife position, Colt in hand, toward the house. An edge of kerosene light ran along the bottom of the front window.

As he opened the front door, Dehner's suspicions were confirmed. The lantern had been placed on the floor. Also on the floor was a body lying face down, a puddle of red had expanded past the blotch of dingy yellow.

As a precaution, Dehner placed two fingers on the corpse's neck to ensure there wasn't a pulse. He then gently turned the body onto its back. "Skeet Jones," the detective said aloud. "If only you could talk right now . . ."

Holstering his gun, Dehner crouched beside the top of the corpse's head and examined the wounds. "Skeet, you were shot at close range, probably an hour or so ago, probably by someone you trusted."

A wave of depression blanketed the detective and, for a few moments, he felt immobile. His eyes stared out the window, "The world is big . . . and most of the time it's dark."

The detective waved both hands as if shooing away his moroseness. He arose, picked up the lantern and left the house by the front door.

Outside he examined the ground around the house as well as he could with only the light from the lantern to work by. "These tracks look fresh. There has been a lot of activity around this place today," the detective said to himself. "Hard to tell how many people have been here."

The back of the house faced a large grassy field. No surprise: the Kimballs ran a ten-head ranch. The field would have been fine for grazing.

One leafy tree occupied the center of the field, billowing over the grass like a decrepit creature of the dark. As Dehner walked toward the tree, his nose confirmed his suspicions. Fresh droppings were scattered under the branches. Someone had tied a horse here and then ridden off after firing two shots at the detective.

Rance would have to wait until sunup to trail his assailant. Keeping the lantern with him, he retrieved his horse and brought it into the barn. He preferred to sleep in the barn and avoid the house and the stench of death which was already filling it.

Dehner gave his bay a rubdown with an empty grain sack he found on the barn floor. A trough ran along one side of the barn with a pump beside it. Dehner found a jug of water in front of the trough and poured it into the head of the pump. With the pump primed he could move the handle up and down to bring fresh water into the trough. He filled his canteen then allowed his bay to slurp up the water.

While the horse drank, Dehner began to refill the water jug. The chore made him feel a bit uneasy. The Kimballs were dead. How long would it be before someone else needed to prime the pump? He finished the job anyway.

He brought the horse that was tethered at the side of the barn inside and also gave it a rubdown and a go at the water. He placed both horses in stalls and provided the animals with feed from a half full bag of oats he located.

His chores finished, Dehner remembered that the saddle bags containing ripped up newspapers were still lying somewhere on the ground between the barn and the house. He would retrieve them in the morning. The detective checked his regular saddle bags. There was enough jerky in the bags to provide breakfast.

The barn contained a lot of loose straw, which made for a decent bed. Some of the straw made a crackling sound as Dehner lay on it, placing his head on his saddle. He thought about Carrie Whiting. The woman was hoping he would apprehend the extortionist and put an end to the threats she had been receiving. So far, he had totally failed.

Dehner closed his eyes as his mind tried to pry up a notion that was itching inside his brain, but whatever it was wouldn't surface. All the detective could bring forth was frustration with himself.

Something soft pressed against his leg. Dehner reached down and petted the cat, which purred contentedly.

"Nice to know I'm making someone happy," he said while sliding into a deep sleep.

Chapter Eighteen

C arrie Whiting finished reading the *Saturday Evening Post* and placed the magazine on her bedside table but she didn't extinguish the lamp. The singer often read herself to sleep but tonight she was too restless and worried for the printed word to be of much help. Why hadn't Rance returned yet? George McLeod had promised to let her know as soon as the detective got back, even if it meant waking her up.

She sighed and fluffed the pillows on her bed for no particular reason. Carrie admitted to herself that her concern for Dehner went deeper than she liked to admit. The self-confession came as a result of a poem she had just read in the magazine.

"Rock Me To Sleep" by Elizabeth Akers Allen was a perennial favorite that the *Post* had originally published in 1860 and had reprinted many times since. The poem had been so popular that it had been set to music and become a standard part of Carrie's repertoire. Carrie began to quietly sing her favorite lines from "Rock Me to Sleep."

Over my heart, in the days that are flown,
No Love like mother-love ever has shown . . .

The singer became quiet, her mind drifting into uneasy thoughts. Would she ever become a mother? She treasured her visits back to the home of Reverend Barton and Emma. Those two people had been so important in her life and she loved them dearly. But, inevitably on those visits, she also encountered former girlfriends from her school days. All of them were now mothers.

"In a few weeks, I'll be twenty," Carrie whispered to herself. "Will I ever have a family of my own?"

Rance Dehner returned to her thoughts. There seemed to be something very special developing between them. And yet, Rance's life was an impossible pursuit. He was seeking redemption for the death of a girl he had loved when he was sixteen.

Carrie again whispered to herself. "You are a wonderful man, Rance Dehner, but not exactly husband material."

The singer closed her eyes and wondered if what she had just said was really true. After all, being the husband of the Songbird of the West would not be easy. It would call for a man who understood people, a man of good judgement and just maybe . . . Rance didn't know the complete story of her upcoming trip to New York. What, if anything, would he do when he found out? Should she even tell him about it?

Carrie opened her eyes as other thoughts flooded her mind. The detective had not yet returned from a very dangerous undertaking. What was happening out there at the Kimball ranch?

Sleep was still a far way off. Carrie remembered there was a short story in the *Saturday Evening Post* she hadn't read. But she decided to forgo the magazine. She got out of bed to fetch her Bible from the open carpet bag where she kept it. Maybe she could find comfort there.

George McLeod stared out the window of his hotel room. There was nothing much to see or hear except the last vestiges of the carnival atmosphere that had followed Carrie's performance. Two men were passed out in the street. Somewhere, out of sight, a drunk shouted angry insipid words at the darkness of night.

Damn it all, where's Dehner?! McLeod thought to himself. Restlessness tormented the agent. He wanted to pace the floor in order to release some energy but was afraid that Carrie, in the room next door, would hear him. No sense in her losing sleep. McLeod remained quiet.

His quietness made him alert to footsteps in the hallway. The agent tensed up. He had checked with Eliab Purvis, the hotel's owner, less than an hour ago. Except for Rance Dehner, all of the guests on the second floor were in their rooms, settled in for the night.

The footsteps could belong to Dehner but George discarded that notion. He had been at the window for at least twenty minutes and hadn't seen the detective ride into Dry River. Of course, Dehner could have come into town by a back way, but why?

George picked up the kerosene lamp which squatted on a small chest of drawers. Patting the gun in his shoulder holster, he moved quietly but hastily to the front door of the room and opened it. A shadow stood in front of Carrie's room. McLeod couldn't tell who it was but the figure appeared to be slipping something over his head.

"Stop right there, mister!" McLeod ordered.

The figure disobeyed orders. He ran back toward McLeod, who partially blocked the path to the stairway. As McLeod began to pull a Remington from its holster the fleeing shadow collided with him. McLeod bumped against the hotel wall and dropped the lantern. The agent holstered the gun and picked up the light before very much kerosene spilled onto the floor. The chimney hadn't broken.

McLeod darted back into his room, doused the light and returned it to the chest of drawers. He then scrambled out into the hallway.

"George, what happened?!" Carrie was standing outside her room wearing a robe.

"Someone tried to break into your room. He's run off. I'm going after him. Get back inside. Don't open the door to anyone but me!"

George ran down the stairway. A quick glance at the front desk revealed there was no one there. McLeod dashed outside, stopped and listened. The heavy pound of running footsteps sounded to his left.

The agent spotted his prey. The man was running past the Silver Crown. "The fool," McLeod said as he again began pursuit. "He's running in a direction where there is still some light."

Passing the Silver Crown, the figure ran down an alley between the saloon and a saddle shop. When McLeod reached the alley he reckoned his adversary wasn't such a fool after all.

A slash of light from a side window in the Silver Crown revealed the outline of several bodies lying in the alley. Nothing unusual about that. After a hard night of drinking a man would often go to an alley beside the saloon to sleep it off. It was safer than passing out in the street, and the law usually left you alone until morning.

Of course, the man who had tried to invade Carrie's room could have run down the alley, hoping the dozing drunks would provide an obstacle course for his pursuer, but McLeod doubted it. The man he was after was not all that fast. His prey was probably posing as one of the drunks, hoping he'd scramble through the alley and continue to chase after a man who was no longer running. Then, the jasper could jump to his feet and vanish into the night.

"I know you're here, mister, and I'm going to find you. Might as well give up now."

There was no response. The agent wasn't really expecting one. He drew his Remington and began to make his way down the alley.

He crouched over the first body he came to but didn't remain there long. Vomit covered the gent's shirt. "You're the genuine article sir," McLeod said. "A real, live, passed out drunk."

The second creature was half-moaning and half-singing with eyes only three quarters closed. McLeod didn't have to crouch down to smell the booze on him.

The agent's nerves became tighter as he approached the third body. This man was positioned face down, away from the window's light. Excitement coursed through George McLeod as he realized the man had a hood of some kind over his head. The hood had been partially pulled up. The snake had tried to pull off his disguise but didn't have time.

George grabbed the hooded figure by his coat collar and pulled him up. Piercing screams came from the captive as McLeod pulled him out of the alley and onto the street where he yanked the burlap bag off his head.

"Laszlo! What the—"

"I play joke on Miss Carrie, she likes jokes."

The agent glanced at the burlap bag. Holes had been punched in it for eyes and there were crude drawings on it. From what McLeod could tell in the darkness, the markings were supposed to make the bag look scary.

"Your jokes aren't funny anymore, Laszlo!" George spoke as he holstered his weapon and poked Laszlo's chest with his index finger. "No more jokes. You are to leave Miss Carrie alone; don't even come inside the hotel."

"I work at the hotel, I work there tonight."

"You're lying! I told Purvis, the owner of the hotel, that you were not to be there while Carrie Whiting was still in town. I'm going to tell you once again, stay away from Miss Carrie. If you try anything again Laszlo, you're going to be sorry, very sorry. Understand?!"

Even in the scant light provided by the night, McLeod could see a complex of emotions twisting across Laszlo's face. The man looked down and said nothing.

George was beginning to feel sorry for the swamper but believed he couldn't allow the sympathy to show. He poked him in the chest again. "Answer me!"

Laszlo's eyes remained downward. "Yes. Understand."

"You'd better understand!" McLeod turned his back on the swamper and stalked off.

Sadness and a certain disgust with himself began to envelop George McLeod as he approached the hotel. The agent really couldn't think of any other way to deal with Laszlo. The man was obsessed with Carrie and could do her harm. The harm would probably be unintentional but still, his chicanery had to be stopped and the kind approach Carrie had employed earlier in the evening had only encouraged the swamper.

"I had to be tough," McLeod said aloud.

But the former boxer recalled how he had hated those in the sport who used their strength to bully others. They seemed to get a thrill from pushing around men who couldn't possibly challenge them. George McLeod wasn't a bully and didn't want to become one.

Entering the hotel, the agent noticed the front desk was still unoccupied. He made his way quickly up the stairs to the second floor. His first stop was at Rance Dehner's room. There was no answer to his knock. He reluctantly approached Carrie's room to convey bad news.

McLeod knocked once on the singer's door, paused and then made five quick knocks. He was following an agreed upon code.

"Come in, George."

McLeod stepped inside and his client closed the door behind him. Even in the wee hours of the morning, Carrie looked beautiful in a thick, scarlet robe. George realized that millions of men throughout the country would envy his being so close to the Songbird of the West. But, as he always did, the agent hastily brushed such thoughts from his mind.

"Laszlo tried to visit you tonight," George held up the burlap bag where Carrie could see the eye holes and the child-like markings. "He thought he was playing another joke."

"Poor man. I pity him, don't you?"

"Yes." McLeod answered truthfully. "But I had to talk tough and scare him a bit. I don't think we'll have any more jokes from Laszlo."

"Is Rance back?"

"No. But there's nothing to be worried about. Rance Dehner is a man who can take care of himself."

Carrie barely managed a hint of a smile as she opened the door for her agent. "Thank you for everything, George."

McLeod stepped into the hallway, then turned back. "Try not to worry, everything is going to be fine."

"You don't really believe that, and neither do I." She started to say something else, then stopped and quietly closed the door.

Laszlo entered the Silver Crown and looked around. Only one table was occupied with a card game. He could do his cleaning now.

The swamper began to stack chairs on top of the tables as he eyed the men playing poker. He recognized all of them. They were nice and wouldn't make fun of him.

But Laszlo still felt miserable as he began to work. *Lies are bad. He tells George a lie about working at the hotel. George is now mad. George tells Carrie that Laszlo is a liar.*

Tears edged out of Laszlo's eyes but no one in the Silver Crown noticed. *Carrie is mad at me.*

The swamper paused and brushed his eyes. *Soon everything is different. Soon comes the big joke. Carrie will like me, will like me a lot.*

Chapter Nineteen

Rance awoke as bright light leaked into the barn. He sat up with the instant knowledge that he had slept longer than planned. The detective quickly made it to his feet and followed the cat to the front doors of the barn.

Removing the wooden bar, Rance opened the double doors allowing the cat to run off in search of breakfast, "Good luck, friend."

Dehner stepped outside and glanced at the sky. He was at least one hour behind his original schedule. The detective reckoned he would eat his jerky while riding. He needed to move out quickly. After all, the guy who shot at him last night did not, in all probability, sleep in.

The detective heard footsteps coming from behind. He turned and ducked as a large red headed man tried to slam a pistol against his head. Dehner burrowed a hard punch into red's mid-section, causing him to double up. Rance's second punch landed right above red's left ear and sent him flopping onto the ground.

The attacker let loose of his gun which landed just inches from his hand. Dehner slammed a foot down on red's wrist as the man reached for his pistol.

"Don't move stranger, put those hands up!" The command came from behind the detective.

Rance did what he was told. The red head gave him a broad, angry smile as he freed his wrist from the detective's boot. "Not sa tough now, are yuh?"

Dehner replied in a monotone. "You're the guy who attacked from behind."

The anger on red's face darkened as he clumsily rose to his feet. "I'll show yuh who can be tough, I'll beat yuh—"

The voice behind Dehner sounded again. "Shut your mouth, Phil! Pick up yore gun, so he cain't grab it, and git yourself over here."

"OK, Simon, OK."

"All right, stranger, turn around, slow."

Dehner once again followed instructions. He kept his voice casual. "I'm not so sure we are strangers, Simon. You look familiar, though I don't think we've been formally introduced."

"Formilly interduced! Yuh sure talk polite-like."

"Simon, I'm always polite when there's a gun pointed at me. It brings out the best in my manners."

"Well, mister, we're gonna learn yuh some more manners at the end of a rope. See, we don't care much for being polite to killers."

"What's going on here?" The harsh shout came from Ezra Brown who was doing a quick walk from the direction of the ranch house. A tall, muscular young man followed behind. The younger man could easily have outpaced Ezra but held back, acknowledging who was the boss.

Dehner recalled where he had seen Simon before. He was one of the six men who had accompanied Ezra Brown when he brought the body of Curt Weldon into town. The man now standing behind Brown was also there. Phil had been somewhere else.

Simon pointed his free hand at Dehner. "We caught this here jasper sneaking 'round the barn."

Brown's eyes penetrated the detective. "I know yuh . . . Dehner the detective from Dallas that's sorta helping out Tal Streeter, or claims he is."

"I'm glad you remember me, Mister Brown."

"Don't be so happy. Yuh ain't in Dallas, Mister Dehner; we got our own ways of doing things here. Skeet Jones is lying dead in the ranch house. Make a case fast and signify why we shouldn't hang you from that tree in the back yard."

As Brown gestured for Simon to holster his gun, Dehner made a quick decision. He had to break a company rule and explain information a client wanted to keep confidential. George McLeod's cheques cleared. But that wouldn't do anyone much good if Rance's feet cleared the ground while his neck was in a noose.

The detective explained his mission to capture

or kill the people who were trying to extort money with the threat of harming Carrie Whiting.

Ezra didn't reject Dehner's account but he looked dubious. "So, jus' where are these saddle bags filled with newspapers yuh say yuh brung?"

Dehner pointed confidently to one side. "Right over there where I dropped them after being shot at."

"Buck." Brown needed only to speak the name of the young man behind him. Buck instantly retrieved the saddle bags and brought them to his boss who glanced at the newspapers inside.

"Yore story kinda makes sense," Ezra spoke as if he were making a concession. "That horse of Skeet's always was nervous and feisty, just like the jasper that owned him."

"Did you know Skeet Jones well, Mr. Brown?" Rance slowly lowered his hands as he spoke. The gesture was hardly threatening. The detective's Colt still lay in its holster which hung from a stall inside the barn.

The rancher sighed deeply before speaking. "Knowed him?! Hell, I own half of that saloon of his."

Dehner was startled and looked it. "Mr. Brown, I wouldn't have pegged you for a man who owned a saloon."

Rance's statement obviously amused the rancher. "Most folks wouldn't. But as a man gits older not much pleasures him anymore. Owning things is all I git much satisfaction from these days, so when Skeet came to me with an offer, I agreed to partner with him in The Silver Crown. He didn't want me to jaw 'bout it none and I was happy to go along, even though I didn't believe his big notions. He was gonna marry Carrie Whiting and she was gonna sing in saloons all over the West that we would own."

"Were you surprised when Carrie Whiting actually came to Dry River?"

"Some," Ezra admitted. "But yuh know I still didn't accept ever thing Skeet Jones tole me. That man jus' worked too hard at looking important. There are times when a man should dress high hat, but Jones dressed like that always: something wrong 'bout a man like that."

Brown looked down and toed the ground for a moment. As he did, Rance noticed the three ranch hands that had accompanied him. They were silent and still, waiting for orders.

The rancher didn't seem to notice. He was inside his own thoughts and having men patiently awaiting his instructions was nothing new.

The rancher's head lifted back up and he eyed Dehner, though he seemed to be speaking half to himself. "The Kimballs were good people: hard working, God fearing. But they jus' wasn't meant for this kind of life. I offered to buy 'em out, tole 'em they'd do better to go back to Ohio. But Bert wanted to own his own place, couldn't take no more factory work. Well, I can unnerstand that, unnerstand it well."

Ezra looked at Buck, who was again standing behind him. A silent communication seemed to pass between them. Ezra Brown hadn't mentioned a family of his own. Dehner wondered if Buck was a surrogate son.

The rancher returned his gaze to Dehner. "Came here this morning to look the place over before riding into town and jawing with Chet Bellamy at the bank. I'm gonna make an offer on this ranch. Besides finding Skeet, I seen Bellamy already had his people out here yesterday. Horses are all gone, so is the furniture and dishes in the house. That would signify all those footprints you saw last night."

Brown paused. He seemed to be wondering whether he should leave well enough alone or surrender to his curiosity. Curiosity won out. "So, you reckon Skeet Jones was the one who hired a gang to help him git ransom money from Miss Whiting. Then, when his plan failed he kept the one hired gun 'round for another try?"

"No," the detective answered. "Skeet was in on some plan or thought he was . . . he probably thought he was a key man. But Skeet was being manipulated and he ended up getting killed."

Dehner pushed his hat back and massaged his forehead. "There was a plan to kidnap Carrie Whiting. Somehow, the schemers found out I was in town to protect Miss Whiting. They didn't want a detective involved so they hired some kid, named Holt Conley, to kill me. Holt tried but failed."

"That don't quite jibe," Brown said. "If they already had a gang ready to kidnap the gal, why not git one of them to kill yuh? From what yuh say, this Holt Conley was pretty green."

"The way I see it, Mr. Brown, Skeet never wanted to actually kill anyone," Rance said. "They hired an outsider to their scheme so Jones wouldn't make a connection between my death and the kidnap plan." The detective paused and then continued. "I'm sure the hired gun who was involved in snatching Carrie Whiting killed Skeet last night. I hope to trail him—"

Ezra threw up both arms in an apologetic gesture. "Guess I ain't been much help to yuh! Go on 'bout yore business. I know Tal will appreciate it, he being without a deputy. I'll see to it that Skeet's body gits to Doc Harding."

"Thanks," Rance said. "And could you tell the sheriff what I'm doing and ask him to pass the word along to George McLeod, Carrie Whiting's agent?"

"Sure." Ezra's voice became lower and very serious. "Watch yourself. This country can produce some bad men, and sounds to me like yore trailing one of the worst."

Chapter Twenty

Dehner saddled his horse quickly and rode from the ranch, but his pace slowed almost immediately. His quarry seemed to have left no trail. After less than an hour, the detective felt completely defeated.

"We're dealing with a killer who is dangerous and smart," Rance said to his horse. "He knows someone is trying to find him and he knows how to make the job tough. Our man seems to be riding on air."

The detective continued his efforts for another half hour with no results. He was now in an area dotted by several small hills. Did the hired gun somehow use those hills to cover his tracks? Dehner's frustration grew more intense.

The clanging sounds of a buckboard came from the other side of one of the hills accompanied by singing. "Oh Susanna, don't you cry for me, cause I'm making Miss Carrie, very happy!"

The voice belonged to Laszlo. Dehner lightly spurred his horse into a lope around the hill. Two large ribbons of dust shot from behind the wagon as it moved along a dusty road.

Dehner moved to the side of the hill for a few moments to give the buckboard a chance to get a reasonable distance ahead of him. Trailing behind Laszlo could be a waste of time. The man did work part time at the mercantile. He could be making a delivery to one of the ranches. But Laszlo seemed to pop up very often in the detective's investigation.

"We're going to follow Laszlo," Dehner again spoke to the bay gelding. "This could be a lucky break, and besides, I don't know what else to do."

Trailing behind Laszlo was easy enough. The wagon created large dust clouds and its driver continued his playful singing.

The buckboard and the singing both stopped at the same time. Dehner pulled up under a clump of trees. He dismounted, tied the bay to one of the tree branches, and yanked his field glasses from the saddle bag.

Using one of the thickest trees as cover, Dehner focused the field glasses on Laszlo. The man was pulling back a tarp that covered the back of the wagon. But he didn't have to pull it far in order to get to the one crate he lifted from the buckboard.

Laszlo carried the crate toward a hill covered by a maze of bushes and weeds. He pushed his way past one of the larger bushes and vanished.

Dehner tensed up. There had to be a cave in that hill. The hired gun could be using the cave as a hideout. Laszlo was bringing the killer food and other supplies.

The detective pegged Laszlo as an innocent pawn. Rance thought back on the song Laszlo had been singing. The man had probably been conned into thinking he was doing Carrie Whiting some kind of favor.

Laszlo pushed his way back into view. He was followed by a burly man, well over six feet, who carried about two hundred pounds and had brown hair which ran almost to his shoulders.

"I think I've found the hired gun," Dehner whispered to himself.

The killer walked with Laszlo to the buckboard. Laszlo began to board the wagon when the hired gun suddenly motioned him down. He talked to the swamper for a moment and Laszlo began to laugh and clap his hands in excitement.

The two men pushed their way past the bushes and reentered the cave. At least, that was how Dehner figured it. The detective sighed deeply and wished he had a better idea of what was going on.

A loud screech shattered his wishing. The screech morphed into a shout for help. The cry came from Laszlo. Maybe his usefulness had ended and the swamper was about to meet death in a remote cave most people didn't know existed.

The screams continued as Dehner untied the bay, mounted and spurred the horse into a fast gallop. As he arrived at the cave entrance, he jumped off the gelding, drew his gun and plowed shoulder first through the thick bushes.

He partially stumbled into a large cave, lit up by two lanterns. Laszlo lay on the ground beside a dying fire. "Help, Mr. Dehner, please!"

The cave was big enough that Rance did not have to stoop down as he moved toward the pleading swamper. "What happened—"

A hard push sent the detective plunging to the ground. He landed face down near Laszlo who grabbed his Colt, jumped up and laughed as he handed it to his long haired companion.

Dehner felt the cold steel of a gun barrel press against the back of his head and heard a low guttural voice. "This part of the joke is done, Laszlo. Make tracks for town. The best part of the joke comes later."

Laszlo jumped up and down with excitement, then ran from the cave. His departure was greeted by a scoff from the man holding a gun on Dehner. "Stupid moron. That joke he's so happy about is gonna put him in a grave."

Rance's face remained pressed against the ground. "You're a real tough guy. Going after people like Laszlo."

"Well now, if that's what's botherin' you, Mr. Rance Dehner, don't you worry no more. See, I'm gonna kill you, too."

Chapter Twenty-One

T he outlaw took a few steps back and gave his prisoner an order. "On your feet, slow like. Don't try no tricks, Rance."

Dehner obeyed the orders and stood facing a man with a Colt .44 in his hand and a smile which reflected both cruelty and curiosity on his face. The detective's gun lay near the front of the cave where his captor had tossed it.

"You seem to know my name, stranger. Why don't you tell me yours? As I recall, we've never been introduced."

"Jake Matson. Ever heard of me?"

"Sure have. According to a lot of lawmen, you're as smart as you are vicious. How did you know I was spying on you?"

Satisfaction crept onto the killer's face. An adversary had just acknowledged that Jake Matson had bested him. "When I was seeing the half-wit off, I noticed one tree branch moving a certain way."

"The way it moves when a horse is nibbling at the leaves," Dehner said. "You're a very observant man, Jake."

Matson's smile broadened. He obviously enjoyed compliments. "A man in my line of work has gotta be ob-ser-vant, otherwise he'll be dead. It was no trouble at all getting the half-wit to help me out. All I hadda do was tell him we was playing a joke on you. That moron loves playing jokes."

Dehner thought it wise to keep the compliments coming. "You don't work cheap, Jake. You have a reputation for charging high. You must be a rich man. Too bad you have to live in a damp cave."

Matson's smile spread wider. "You're right 'bout me being rich. Hideouts like this jus' come with the job. You should understand, Rance. See, I've heard a lot about you, too. A pal even pointed you out to me at a eating hole in Dallas a year or so back. You've put friends of mine in jail and in boot hill."

For the second time that morning, Dehner slowly lowered his hands. His captor expressed no objections. The detective matched Matson's mock friendly voice. "You know, I'd like to say that it was nothing personal putting those jaspers where I put them. But that wouldn't be the truth. I just don't care much for your friends."

Jake smirked. He seemed to be genuinely enjoying the conversation. "Yup. I keep company with pretty rude characters. They wouldn't impress a fine citizen like yourself. See, I know you by more than jus' repetation. Laszlo's been talking big 'bout you, how you saved him from a bully. Seems you're a right nice fella."

"My mother brought me up right. Made me go to Sunday School and learn the golden rule. 'Do unto others' and all that."

"I didn't spend much time in Sunday School, myself."

"Doesn't surprise me."

"I knowed you an me would meet up some day, Rance. And, to be factual, it's happened at a right convenient time."

"How do you figure?"

"I got me in a right crazy sitcheation. Seemed like easy money at first, but I gotta admit, I was a fool to go along with the whole scheme. See, I got hired by jaspers who thought they was real smart. Them's the kind a man should stay far from. I should stick to the type who jus' wants you to kill and get the hell outta town. I'm killing Laszlo in a few days. The fool thinks he's going to Dallas to see the Songbird of the West. But for right now . . . ever one says you're a smart detective. I hafta know jus' how much of all this you've got figured."

"And after I tell you everything I know you're going to kill me."

Jake shrugged his shoulders. "You shoulda reckoned you'd end up dead from a bullet, given your calling. But, stuff like that ain't supposed to bother a fine Christian gent like yourself. Ain't there some mansion waiting for you after you get put in a pine box?"

The hired gun laughed at his remarks, then continued. "Sit down an' make yourself at home." Matson pointed to an empty crate in front of Dehner. He moved around to the other side of the hot embers which had a coffee pot hanging over them.

"The coffee must be getting cold by now, I'll heat it up." He picked up a near empty bottle of kerosene and poured the remaining contents on the fire which flared up to a modest degree. Dehner took note of the two lanterns which hung in the cave on each side of the entrance. Jake Matson was a man who liked warmth and light.

The detective also noted that there were three wooden crates in the cave. One lay on the other side of the fire and was used as a chair by Matson after he tossed the kerosene onto the red embers. The other crate sat to the left of Dehner and was close enough that Dehner could tell it contained an array of boxes and bottles: the crate Laszlo had carried in.

Jake Matson looked a bit more relaxed as he pointed his .44 at Dehner from the other side of the fire. "Now, while our java heats up, tell me how you got this thing figured, Mr. Detective."

"Well, at first, I couldn't quite figure out the role Skeet Jones played in all of this."

"Why's that?"

"Skeet saw Carrie Whiting as his ticket to wealth and glory, but I think it went beyond that.

Skeet Jones adored Carrie and may have loved her. In a strange way, Carrie Whiting dominated Skeet's life."

"I don't quite follow you."

"Seven years ago, Skeet rescued Carrie from a terrible situation," Dehner continued. "Since that time, he has been trying to recreate that scene. He wanted desperately for people to know him as the man who rescued the Songbird of the West. I think I've finally figured out how his desires got him killed."

"Keep talking."

"Skeet got money from Carrie Whiting, but he needed more . . . he always needed more money for his big schemes. So, he partnered with some folks who agreed to help Jones with what he considered a terrific plan."

"And jus' what was this here plan?"

"Skeet got Carrie to come to Dry River. A gang was hired to kidnap her. But, the kidnapping would be phony. Skeet would rescue Carrie from the outlaws. Of course, it would be staged. The bad men would all get away but Carrie would be safe. In Skeet's mind, Carrie Whiting would love the man who had saved her a second time. She would marry him and spend years singing at saloons Skeet owned."

Jake Matson's smile altered a bit. He appeared genuinely impressed with Rance's deductions. "Yup, Skeet had him some pretty crazy notions.

So, tell me what happened next, Mr. Detective?"

"Skeet was gullible. He partnered with some people who wanted the kidnapping to be real."

Matson nodded his head. "Hell, why go along with Skeet's idea which, even if it worked, would only bring in money slow like over several years? And the jaspers actually doing the dirty work would never see the big money. By really kidnapping the gal, you could get a ten thousand dollar ransom real quick like. The hired guns who snatched her could get a nice cut as could ever body else. Forget Skeet's crazy notions."

"Skeet's partners had a lot more in mind than just ignoring his ideas," Dehner said. "They couldn't allow him to live. He'd never let Carrie Whiting really be kidnapped. He'd blow apart their chance at collecting a fat ransom. As I see it, Skeet was to act out his phony rescue the night following the kidnapping. When he showed up at the Kimball ranch he would be killed."

A low rumble came into Jake Matson's voice. "You surely messed up things, Rance. Don't know how you reckoned we was at the Kimball ranch. But instead of Skeet getting killed the second night four of us got killed the first night. Me being the only one who escaped."

"But you and the folks you worked with still had some hopes of getting your hands on serious money."

"And how were we going to do that?"

"You were a key man in the back-up plan, Jake. You snuck up on George McLeod late one night and demanded three thousand dollars in protection money. That's a far cry from ten thousand, but still not bad, and the money could be raised locally in Dry River. There was another important part of the plan."

The anger grew more intense in the voice of Jake Matson. "And jus' what was this here other im-por-tant part?"

"You convinced Skeet Jones he'd have a chance of playing hero in a different charade. He was going to stop you from collecting the money from George McLeod and run you off. Your real intent was to kill Skeet before McLeod arrived. You'd then kill McLeod and get the loot. The law would find Jones and McLeod dead and the money gone."

"Bullseye, Mr. Detective. Poor Skeet thought that this time a phony drama would make him a hero to his pretty songbird at long last."

"Poor Skeet was just too much trouble. He was probably already upset about the stage coach driver and the shotgun being killed. You must have convinced him that those deaths were unintended,—one of those crazy things that goes wrong. Murdering Skeet also rid you of a jasper you were supposed to share the money with."

"You had to go and get your fingers in that plan too, Rance. You spoiled ever thing. When you showed up, I knew you didn't bring the money with you. That ain't the way your type works. There was nothing for me to do but get out. Well, Mr. Detective, now you're gonna find out how my type works." The thumb on Matson's gun hand began to move. He was getting ready to cock the .44.

"How about that coffee you promised me, Jake?"

Matson paused and Dehner knew what was running through the gunny's mind. A hired gun lives in his reputation: a reputation as vital to him as to the people who pay for his services. To deny Dehner the coffee would make him look yellow; it would appear to be an act of cowardice that would lower himself in his own mind.

"Sure Rance, some folks say a cup of java is a good way to end the day. In your case it's gonna be a good way to end your life."

Both men stood up. Keeping his .44 on Dehner, Matson picked up two tin cups from the ground and placed them on the crate where he had been sitting. He removed the coffee pot from the overhang which arched over the fire and began to pour.

"From now on, I'm sticking to the easy jobs. Jus' kill some jasper and leave town . . ."

As Matson babbled on Dehner took a quick look at the crate which Laszlo had delivered. There were several cans of food, some coffee, a box of ammunition and what appeared to be three bottles of whiskey. Jake Matson was a man who enjoyed his drink. The detective took a more careful look at the bottles. The liquid in one of them was not amber colored and had been clumsily marked with a K.

The third bottle contained kerosene! Someone had used an empty whisky bottle to send Jake Matson the kerosene he needed for his lanterns and fires. Dehner had employed the coffee ploy to stall for time. He now used that time to frantically construct a plan.

Not much of a plan but it might be enough to keep me from that pine box and mansion for a while, Dehner mused.

"Here you go, Mr. Detective," Jake handed Rance a cup of coffee across the fire with his left hand. "Not as good as what you get in them fancy restaurants in Dallas or Denver, but I ain't charging you nothing for it." Matson's gun remained fixed on Dehner.

Rance accepted the java and took a sip of it. "Tastes fine, but you know some folks like cream in their coffee. Me, I prefer something a little stronger. He tilted his head toward the full crate. "You got some fine whiskey in there. Mind sharing a bit?"

"Be my guest."

Dehner crouched down beside the crate, placing his coffee on the ground in front of him.

He reached down and pretended to rip away a seal while pulling out a cork from the bottle that contained kerosene. He pulled the bottle out of the crate by the neck and poured some of its contents into his coffee cup. The detective kept the bottle as far out of sight of his captor as he could without arousing suspicion.

Remaining in a crouch, he pretended to drink from his cup. "I'll have to say this: at least I'm being killed by a man with good taste in whiskey. No rot gut for you, Jake. You drink only the best. Say, can I spike your coffee?"

"Don't mind if you do."

Matson's .44 remained fixed on Dehner. The killer wasn't taking anything for granted but his confidence was running high. That was the best Rance could hope for.

Dehner buoyed out of his crouch and, coffee in one hand and bottle in the other, he ambled toward the fire with a smile on his face. Matson held out his cup. Rance threw kerosene onto his captor, poured the remaining liquid into the fire and jumped backwards.

Flames soared upwards as hell erupted in the cave. Jake Matson screamed in agony, pounding an arm against the red tentacles that now enveloped his clothes. He dropped to the ground and began to roll hoping earth would extinguish the fire which lashed at his body.

Dehner had also hit the ground. He rolled

toward the crate, grabbed the box of ammunition and threw bullets into the fire.

Explosions sounded in the cave. Red stars seem to shoot from the fire as the sound echoed off the stone walls. Panic gripped Jake Matson, who desperately hoped he had completely extinguished the flames on his clothes. He looked at his right hand. Yes, he had not let go of the Colt .44.

Matson stood up and barked a shot through the fire and in the direction of where he thought Dehner was lying. As he did, Matson felt the red monster return and sink its fiery claws into his left leg.

The gunman shouted a string of curses which almost sounded like a plea to heaven for mercy. The plea went unanswered. Fire encircled his leg. Jake Matson let out a loud screech as he bolted out of the cave.

Dehner could hear the rustling of thickets as Matson pushed through the bushes that covered the cave entrance. The detective carefully got back onto his feet. He bowed into a jackknife position as he advanced toward his gun. Picking up the weapon, he could hear his adversary moaning not far from the cave entrance. The moan seemed to signal relief. Jake had finally put out the fire that had threatened to kill him.

Dehner quietly but quickly moved away from his position. Matson's panic had subsided. He would remember where he had tossed Dehner's gun.

Rance lay on the ground close to where Matson only a few moments before had frantically fought his battle against a red devil. Pieces of singed clothing dotted the area.

The detective thought he heard the sound of stumbling footsteps. Jake Matson was making an escape. Dehner faced a treacherous dilemma. Matson was a dangerous killer and wounded, he could be even more dangerous. But a hired gun like Jake might give some thought to running off Dehner's horse. It could take the detective hours to retrieve the bay. Hours that could cost a life.

Gun in hand, Rance advanced to the cave entrance and plowed through the bushes. Outside, he looked about for Matson but his adversary was nowhere in sight. The detective then glanced toward the grove of trees. The bay had meandered about and then returned to feast on the grass.

Hoof beats pounded from the other side of the hill. Jake Matson suddenly rode into view. Part of his upper body and legs were exposed. The skin in places looked shriveled and charred. He was riding in the opposite direction of Dry River.

The gunney stopped his horse and fired a shot in Dehner's direction, more to back the detective off than to hit him. "We'll meet again Mr. Detective!" He raked his horse viciously and the animal galloped off.

A cold blooded killer was seriously wounded. This was a good time to capture or kill him and maybe save some lives down the road. But Jake Matson was no longer a threat to Carrie Whiting and Dehner's first obligation was to his client and an innocent in Dry River who faced death immediately.

The detective ran to his steed and quickly mounted. He only had to rake his spurs lightly to prod the horse into a fast run. As the bay gelding carried him to Dry River, he thought about those final words the killer had shouted at him.

Yes, some day he would face Jake Matson again, but right now there were other killers that needed justice's wrath.

Chapter Twenty-Two

Carrie Whiting's face was ashen. The singer's hands gripped the arms of the small chair she was sitting in. Carrie looked as if she were bracing for an assault. "Skeet was . . . well . . . he was confused. But . . . at heart . . . Skeet wanted to be good and . . . I owe him so very much. In a way he really did save my life. I wish . . ."

The young woman stopped speaking. She picked up the handkerchief which had been lying on her lap and buried her face in it.

George McLeod sighed deeply. "Dehner, can't we talk about all this later?"

"No!" Carrie returned the handkerchief to her lap. Anger seemed to give her new energy. "Rance knows who is behind these killings. We've got to do all we can to stop them."

George McLeod sighed again and shrugged his shoulders. "OK, Dehner, what exactly do you have in mind?'

Dehner, McLeod and Sheriff Tal Streeter were crowded into Carrie's hotel room. Dehner had called the meeting immediately upon returning to Dry River. The hotel room seemed the safest location. Rance had a notion that the killers were keeping an eye on them as best they could. Carrie walking to the sheriff's office might put them on the alert. But the hotel was a normal part of the sheriff's rounds.

"We have to move today," the detective said. "I'm convinced Laszlo's life is in danger. He has been used as a pawn and now he knows too much."

"You're kinda goin' too fast for this simple lawdog," Tal Streeter said. "I know yuh jus' poured out the whole story, but could yuh start again at the beginin'?"

Rance understood the sheriff's confusion. The detective had just hastily spilled everything about the case. He needed to back up.

"Laszlo was the perfect pawn," Dehner responded. "His main job is as a swamper at the Silver Crown. But he does odd jobs all over town. He works at the mercantile and the hotel now and then. With a big crowd in town to see Carrie, no one would pay much notice to Laszlo doing chores at the hotel."

The sheriff nodded his head. "So, yuh say it was Laszlo who put the doll with a knife stickin' out of it in Miss Whiting's room?"

"Yes, he honestly thought he was playing a joke. Of course, the real motive behind the doll was to scare us into thinking that even though she was being guarded, Carrie could be harmed. Therefore, extortion needed to be paid.

But the people who put Laszlo up to it couldn't completely control him."

McLeod took the cigar out of his mouth and pointed it at Rance. "Meaning, Laszlo dressing up like a ghost and charging at Carrie during her performance was all his idea."

"Yes. Laszlo must have figured that anyone who thought a doll with a knife through it was funny would find a ghost to be hilarious."

Carrie Whiting lightly caressed her forehead. "I'm afraid I encouraged him to feel that way. After all, I complimented Laszlo on his ghost act. I got the crowd to applaud him. No wonder he decided to put on a silly mask and try to play another joke on me last night."

"Don't feel bad, Miss Whiting." There was genuine admiration in Tal Streeter's voice. "Yuh handled that crowd very well. Yuh probably stopped a riot."

The sheriff turned his head to Dehner. "Are you sure Laszlo is in danger now?"

"Matson had a plan to kill Laszlo. Soon, the people who hired Jake Matson will realize he's gone, but Laszlo still knows far too much—"

"So, they'll kill him!" Streeter said. "Hell, they might do it tonight!"

McLeod once again pointed his cigar at Dehner; this time an ash fell off. The agent didn't seem to notice. "I find it hard to buy this notion of yours about the people behind all these killings."

"I agree," Carrie said. "I mean, Felix and Andrea Murphy! They seem like such harmless people."

Dehner gave the woman a kind smile before he replied. "They didn't seem so harmless the first time you met them, seven years ago."

Carrie replied with a startled expression. She said nothing.

"Something has been eating at me since Tal and I had a conversation with the Murphys concerning the Carrie Whiting dolls," Dehner said. "Last night when I was sharing a barn with a cat, I tried to think of what it was, but it still escaped me until I was riding back to Dry River. Carrie, has any newspaper or magazine article specifically mentioned the date of your birthday?"

"No . . . a few have mentioned my age . . . nineteen."

"And you are going to be twenty reasonably soon."

"Yes . . . October Third. But how did you know my birthday was coming up?"

"Andrea Murphy told me. While the sheriff and I were talking to the Murphys, Andrea said you weren't 'quite twenty yet'. That implied she knew your birthday was near."

The singer looked confused. "But how would . . ." The confusion vanished. "Andrea Murphy was there. . . ."

Dehner cut in. "Seven years ago, the people we now call Felix and Andrea Murphy owned Bob's Place, a brothel located in another town. Felix used to call himself Bob Hoover—"

Now it was Carrie's turn to cut in. "He had a beard then! I don't remember much about the woman except her long hair which, of course, she cut!"

Carrie Whiting got out of her chair and began to pace about the room. "They'd remember that terrible night as vividly as I do. They would even remember the date and that it was my birthday."

"Exactly," Dehner agreed. "They probably had to vamoose the next day. Having the town's wealthiest citizen killed in their establishment didn't give them much of a future in that place."

Tal Streeter seemed to retreat into himself for a moment, as if searching his mind for past actions. "The Murphys arrived in Dry River 'bout three years ago. Got no idea as to where they been before that. They wasn't rich but seemed to have money in their pockets . . . they had them enough dinero to buy the mercantile."

"What about Skeet Jones?" Dehner asked.

"He was different altogether. Hit Dry River 'bout a year and a half back, pretended to be a high stakes gambler. I didn't buy it at first but then I sorta changed my mind."

"Why?" Dehner asked.

"Well, he had him enough money to buy the Silver Crown."

"Skeet fooled a lot of people with that move," Dehner responded. "He got some of the money from Carrie and the rest from Ezra Brown, who was his silent partner."

The detective suddenly paused. Carrie Whiting understood why. "This is no time for courtesy, Rance. Say what you need to about Skeet Jones."

Dehner smiled wistfully at the singer and continued. "When you gave Skeet money to help him buy the saloon, you probably ignited some wild dreams in a man who was already a dreamer."

George McLeod's face crunched up. "I don't understand."

"Skeet connected with the Murphys," Dehner answered. "They recognized each other. And of course, with Carrie's picture in all the newspapers and magazines, the Murphys had long ago figured out that Carrie Whiting was the girl they had called Angela the Angel. They knew Skeet could get Carrie to come to Dry River, where they could grab her and get a fortune in a ransom. Of course, they had to set up Skeet for a double cross."

The sheriff's face expressed no emotion as he spoke. "So, why'd they have to kill Curt Weldon?"

Dehner softened his voice. "Curt was killed because he was a deputy."

The lawman looked confused. "What?"

"After their first plan failed, Felix and Andrea Murphy panicked. They had one more chance at getting big money. Extortion. They had to put a real scare into Carrie and George."

McLeod let out a loud curse. "Ramming a knife through a Carrie Whiting doll and leaving it on Carrie's bed wasn't enough. They had to kill Curt Weldon and put a note in his pocket, letting us know that they were savvy about a deputy rescuing Carrie years ago."

"Yes," Dehner said. "Skeet must have told them about his encounter with Carrie when she was fifteen."

"Felix Murphy killed my deputy?"

"Probably," Dehner answered. "Judging from Curt's wounds. I think the Murphys got Jake Matson to ambush Curt. Matson came to your office early that morning posing as one of Ezra Brown's ranch hands. He told you a lie about Ezra Brown being shot at. With everything that was going on in Dry River, they figured you'd tell Curt to look into it so you could remain in town."

"They sure had me pegged," the lawman said.

Dehner continued: "But when Matson returned, they found out that their hired gun had forgotten to leave a note incriminating Skeet Jones in Curt's pocket. Felix Murphy went to the site of the ambush and found Curt by Stony creek struggling for life. Murphy ended the struggle with a bullet to Curt's head, and then left the note."

Tal Streeter briefly massaged the back of his neck. "They must have reckoned that when Skeet turned up dead, this lawdog would figger Jones was the main culprit and whoever got away with the loot was a small time crook Skeet had hired to help him."

A moment of silence followed, which Carrie Whiting broke. "These are horrible people. We've got to do something to stop them."

"We are," Rance said. "And Carrie, we will need your help to do it."

Chapter Twenty-Three

Sheriff Tal Streeter walked down the board-walk as perspiration collected on his forehead. Still, he felt good about the afternoon heat. Most folks were inside now doing what they could to stay out of the sun. Otherwise, Carrie Whiting appearing on the town's main street would stir up a swarm of people.

He stopped, took off his hat, and made an elaborate production of wiping his forehead. Tal looked down the street to where Rance Dehner was also taking off his hat. That was a signal. Everything was fine on Dehner's side. It was time to move.

Less than an hour had passed since the meeting at the hotel. Since then, Dehner had discreetly checked out the mercantile and the group had finalized their plans. The plan was simple enough, which the lawman figured was how it should be.

Streeter put his hat back on and tried to appear casual as he made his way toward the mercantile. The sheriff mused on the fact that he had known Felix and Andrea for over three years . . . or thought he had. He wondered if maybe a lot of people in Dry River weren't what they appeared to be. Were many of the people he met every day toting around some terrible secrets?

"Whoa!" Streeter whispered to himself. "Yore a small town lawdog, yuh ain't no philosopher."

The lawman turned and began to stroll down the wide alley between the mercantile and Earl's Gun Shop. Dehner had informed him that Andrea and Laszlo were in the back of the store loading a buckboard. Streeter heard voices confirming what the detective had reported.

"Hurry up, Laszlo, yore slower than molasses!"

"I feel tired. This is real delivery, not make believe. Lots of things to put in wagon and the sun is hot—"

"OK, OK, be careful when yuh hitch them horses to the buckboard, do it right!"

Streeter caught Laszlo's remark about a "real delivery." When he took supplies out to Jake Matson, Laszlo drove a wagon with a tarp on the back covering mostly empty crates. Since Laszlo made deliveries to various ranches, the sight of him driving a buckboard out of town would pretty much go unnoticed.

Streeter arrived at the end of the alley and the back of the store. Andrea was fussing with the tarp while Laszlo was hitching four horses to the wagon. Behind them was a small corral and barn; the back door to the mercantile stood wide open in a vain struggle against the heat.

"Afternoon, Andrea." The sheriff touched his hat with two fingers.

"Why . . . afternoon Tal! Looks like yuh gone loco, doin' a round on a hot day like this."

The woman sounded friendly but Streeter could tell she was working at it. "I'm doin' what I gotta do to make a livin'," Streeter moved closer to the open door as he spoke. "Jus' like you folks."

Laszlo laughed hard as he continued to work on the harnesses. "The sheriff is right. We have to make living."

"Well, yuh don't hafta worry none about us, Tal. It's too blasted hot for anyone to try a hold up. Tell yuh what, as soon as . . ."

Andrea stopped speaking and took a step toward the back door. Through the open doorway she could see a storage room and most of the store's counter. She watched her husband step off of a stool. Andrea's vision was limited to one side of the store's only customer but a profile was all she needed. "Well, I'll be . . . seems we got ourselfs a very important customer . . . Miss Carrie Whiting."

"Guess she reckons it's all right to come out now with most folks stayin' inside," the sheriff said.

Andrea continued to stare through the doorway. Nickering horses caused her to glance sideways.

"Be nice, be nice." Laszlo was trying to pacify the restless animals.

"Tal, I know yuh got a round to do but could yuh help that poor half wit," Andrea spoke in a whisper. "He can't seem to get that buckboard hitched up proper like. Last week, the horses broke loose while he was makin' a delivery to the Jameson ranch."

"Sure."

Streeter felt gratitude for the request. He needed a reason to remain where he was for a few more minutes. The sheriff smiled as he approached Laszlo. He knew the man would resent being helped. Like a child, Laszlo would insist that he could do it himself.

"Yuh know, Laszlo, horses are like people, they get kinda fussy in the hot weather."

Laszlo chuckled at Streeter's remark, which made the sheriff happy. He didn't stay happy long. Something hard slammed against his head. Tal cursed himself inwardly for turning his back on Andrea. The sheriff staggered about trying to keep his balance. He tried to shout out a warning to Dehner but it came out as weak cry.

Streeter reached for one of the horses in an effort to steady himself. But Tal's vision was now fuzzy and his hand seemed to pass through the animal. The lawman dropped to the ground.

Through blurred vision, the sheriff watched Andrea hug Laszlo. No, she wasn't hugging the swamper, she was placing a hand over his mouth and whispering something to him.

Tal Streeter fought the urge to at least try to get back onto his feet. He was hopelessly weak. If Andrea Murphy realized he was still conscious she would give him another whack on the head and send him into darkness.

The sheriff closed his eyes and remained still as Andrea removed the gun from his holster.

Chapter Twenty-Four

Rance Dehner put his hat back on as he watched Tal make his way toward the mercantile. The detective hurriedly reentered the hotel, almost running as he made his way to the second floor and Carrie Whiting's room.

"Tal and I just exchanged signals," Dehner spoke to both the singer and her agent. "We need to get moving. Carrie, you go first. George and I will be just a minute behind you."

Carrie nodded her head and walked at a fast pace out of the room and out of the hotel. Pausing for a brief moment on the boardwalk she noted that luck seemed to be on her side. The boardwalks on both sides of the street were barren of people.

As she crossed the street and made her way to the store, Carrie reflected on the many individuals who would still be alive if she had never come to Dry River. "I need to be a part of this," she said under her breath. "I need to help bring these terrible people to justice."

The young woman slowed her pace as she entered the mercantile. She smiled at Felix Murphy who was standing on a small stool stocking the shelves behind the counter and looked shocked to see her.

"Good afternoon, Mr. Murphy."

"Why . . . good afternoon, Miss Whiting," the store owner laughed nervously. "I'm surprised to see you here."

"I just had to get out of my room for a few minutes." She pointed to a line of four jars on the counter. "Even the Songbird of the West can get a sweet tooth now and again."

Murphy laughed as he got off the stool and stepped toward the jars. "Which would you like?" He laughed again.

Carrie widened her eyes and stared silently at Felix Murphy.

Her acting fooled the town's mayor. "Anything wrong, Miss Whiting?"

"You can shave your beard off, Bob Hoover, but you couldn't change that strange laugh of yours: four straight guffaws in a row, fired like gun shots."

The storekeeper laughed again, this time out of habit. "I don't know what yore talking 'bout."

"Yes you do, Mr. Murphy or whatever your name is. You enjoy playing with names, don't you? After all, you changed my name to Angela the Angel. Some angel you planned to make of me."

"That was a long time ago. Let's jus' forget it. Get outta this store."

"Oh, I'll leave. In fact I think I'll head for the sheriff's office. I think he might be interested in some of the background I can provide him about the mayor of Dry Creek."

Murphy's eyes narrowed. "You think you're better than anyone else, don't you, Miss Carrie Whiting? You should have all the money, let everyone else struggle to jus' survive."

Carrie's voice conveyed no emotion. "You are the one who planned my kidnapping. You and your wife. After that failed, you tried to extort three thousand dollars—"

"Yep, that's right! You're real smart, Miss Whiting, a little too smart," Felix Murphy began to reach under the counter.

"Hands up, your honor!" Rance stormed into the mercantile. George McLeod was right behind him. Both men held guns in their right hands.

"Step back from the counter!" Dehner ordered. While still keeping an eye on Felix Murphy, the detective shouted, "You can bring Mrs. Murphy in now, Tal!"

"Mrs. Murphy can come in all by herself!" Andrea Murphy stepped inside, holding the sheriff's Colt. "I heard enough of what that singer said to know somethun was up, somethun bad. Drop them guns ontuh the floor gents, real nice like, or I send a bullet right in tuh the pretty face of the Songbird of the West."

Dehner and McLeod did what they were told.

"Pick up them guns!" Andrea ordered her husband. "We gotta act fast."

Felix scrambled from behind the counter and scooped up the weapons. "Whata we need these for?"

"We gotta kill these here folks, and Tal Streeter too." Andrea crunched up her face as if finalizing plans. "This here is goin' tuh be our story. Carrie Whiting comes in the store. Dehner comes in behind her and gets fresh. The agent guy runs in and starts arguin' with Dehner. It ends in a shoot-out. The gal gets herself killed in the crossfire. Tal Streeter hears the ruckus while doin' a round and barges in jus' in time tuh take him a bullet."

"Nobody will believe that," Carrie Whiting said.

"Shore they will, sweet thing," Andrea responded. "Don'tcha wish the kidnappin' plan had worked? The mayor and me woulda got us ten thousand dollars and yuh would still live to sing in New York and all them other big places."

Andrea shifted her eyes to her husband. "Bring them guns here, we—"

"Not nice! Not nice!" Laszlo came running in from the back of the store.

"Laszlo listen to me—"

Laszlo stood inches from Andrea, facing her directly. "We not play joke. Sheriff Streeter is really hurt." Laszlo raised both of his hands which were covered with blood. "Sheriff is really bleeding but he still talk, tell truth."

Felix Murphy now stood beside his wife,

keeping a gun pointed at the three prisoners. But the storekeeper was allowing his wife to handle Laszlo. Something she had apparently done well in the past.

"Laszlo, listen tuh me." The woman's voice sounded increasingly desperate. "I kin tell yuh jus' how—"

"Leaving doll on bed is not nice, sheriff tell me so." Laszlo turned and bolted toward the singer. "Miss Carrie, sheriff say you not really think doll on bed is funny. Is that right?"

"Yes, Laszlo, the sheriff is right."

Both of the swamper's hands became fists as he turned and once again faced the Murphys. "Liars!" He charged at the couple.

Carrie Whiting, her agent and Dehner looked at Andrea Murphy to see what she would do. All three of them were shocked when Felix Murphy almost casually raised one arm and fired a shot at Laszlo.

The swamper screamed in pain as his body twirled, then plunged to the floor. Dehner took advantage of the commotion to jump over the store's counter. He grabbed the six gun which lay on a shelf under the counter.

There was a fast exchange of bullets as Dehner and the storekeeper fired at each other and missed. Andrea glanced at George McLeod who was hustling his client out of the store.

"Our plans are ruined," the woman said to her

husband. "We gotta run quick." The woman fired a shot at Laszlo who screamed loudly. Almost as an afterthought, Andrea flamed a bullet in Rance's general direction, then the couple made a fast exit out the back of the store.

Holstering the gun he had found, Dehner again jumped over the counter. The detective then did exactly what Andrea had hoped. Instead of taking off after Andrea and Felix, he crouched over Laszlo.

"Not nice, not nice," the swamper's head moved from side to side as pain racked his body.

Carrie and George came rushing back into the store. They both crouched beside Laszlo. "How is he?" the singer asked.

"He took a bullet in the left shoulder," came Dehner's clipped reply. "Andrea tried to put a second bullet into him but she missed."

Felix Murphy's voice blared from behind the store, followed by thundering hoof beats and the clattering of the buckboard.

"They're gettin' away." Tal Streeter stumbled into the store.

Dehner buoyed out of his crouch, ran to the lawman and helped him into a chair across from the counter. "Careful, Tal, you may have a concussion."

"Nope," the sheriff's voice was weak but clear. "Andrea hit hard, but my noggin is even harder. I didn't pass out. Talked some sense to Laszlo, shook him loose from those fool notions 'bout a joke. Hope I didn't get the poor jasper killed."

"What's goin' on?" A short, portly man stood in the front doorway. He pointed with his thumb to the gun shop next door. "I was snoozin' in the back of my store when . . . Carrie Whiting!"

Streeter's voice lifted to a loud shout. "Earl, get the doctor, now!"

"Yes, Sheriff!" Earl smiled at Carrie, then took off.

The singer spoke softly to the lawman. "Is there a well out back?"

"Yes, near the barn."

"I'll get some water, you and Laszlo need it." Carrie hastily departed through the back door.

Laszlo had been moaning in a sing-song manner. His moans became louder.

"Try to relax, friend," George McLeod said. "The doc is on his way."

Dehner realized everything in the store was under control. "I'll also be on my way, there are two people I need to meet up with."

As Dehner ran from the mercantile to the hotel, he saw Earl running to the doctor's place. The shots had prodded some stragglers out onto the boardwalk. A few people shouted questions at Earl but the gun shop owner ignored them.

So did Rance, paying no attention to babble coming at him from the handful of people in

191

front of the hotel. He untied his horse from the hitch rail, mounted and rode out of town in an increasingly fast lope which turned into a gallop.

About fifteen minutes out of Dry River, he spotted a moving dust cloud. The detective pulled his bandanna up over his nose. The bay cooperated with Dehner as they gained on the buckboard. In fact, the bay was enjoying the run. The horse's body seemed to unfold and spread out over the road as they drew closer to the Murphys.

But Rance slowed the horse as they began to go up toward a mesa. The detective was now close enough to the buckboard to notice its awkward maneuvers. The wagon swayed across the road in occasional fits of erratic motions. The buckboard resembled a wounded bear moving at a fast pace but in a swerving, unbalanced manner.

Dehner slowed his animal even more as the road began to narrow. The detective had ridden over this road yesterday. He knew soon it would become narrower, running over a steep drop.

A shot fired from the wagon. The detective bent over onto the bay's neck. The bullet whined harmlessly past him.

Another shot followed with the same result. Sharp whip cracks cut the air as Felix Murphy pushed his horses mercilessly.

As if in response to the brutality, the four animals broke loose from the buckboard as the wagon tilted sideways, then tumbled and skidded down the long rocky slope. It smashed against a large boulder, making an explosive sound which was followed by a woman's scream. The scream was brief.

Dehner pulled up his bay as the crashing sound of the wagon subsided. Flying gravel rained down around the wreckage as dust billowed up like smoke from wildfire.

A huge dust cloud now blocked Dehner's view of the wagon. He dismounted and ground tethered his horse. The detective drew the gun he had grabbed from under the counter of the mercantile and made his way cautiously down the slope.

The dust cloud became increasingly thick as Rance neared the wagon. A sound, something between a laugh and a cry, came from the wreckage. Heavy, uncertain footsteps began to weave toward Dehner.

Felix Murphy stumbled into view. He and Dehner were in a cocoon of spiraling dust which seemed to cut them off from the rest of the world. Murphy carried Rance's Colt in his right hand but had it pointed at the ground.

"That moron didn't hitch up the horses right!" Felix gave his familiar laugh but now it was high pitched, sounding almost like a succession of squeaks. "You'd think jus' once he coulda' got it right!"

A stream of curses came from Murphy as he continued to stagger about. "Andrea kept blabberin' 'bout how she could handle the idiot. Well now she's dead!"

"Drop the gun, Felix."

The storekeeper ignored the order. He continued to meander in front of the wagon, speaking in a pleading voice as if addressing a celestial court. "Andrea and me, we wanted to get rich. We tried runnin' whorehouses, tried in a few places but somethun' always went wrong. Came to Dry River and bought the mercantile. Yuh know what ruined that?"

Dust began to settle on Murphy, like a shroud of death. Rance spoke quietly as if at a graveside service. "No, you tell me, Felix."

"Selling newspapers and magazines! Ever one of them damn things made a big deal over Carrie Whiting. The Songbird of the West! Hell, she's the one that ruined the best chance we had of getting rich! That fool Skeet Jones killed the richest man in Calhoun, Texas over that girl. Andrea and me had to leave a town that was making us wealthy. Never got that close to being rich again."

Dehner felt increasingly edgy. He was staring into the darkest corner of a man's soul. Still, he was driven to probe further. "What did you think when Skeet Jones turned up in Dry River?"

Felix Murphy suddenly stopped pacing. After

a few moments of silence, he began to speak as moisture pooled at the corners of both eyes. "We thought our luck had finally changed. Andrea and me recognized him right off, before he recognized us. He started bragging the moment he knowed who we was. Jawed on and on 'bout how he could bring Carrie Whiting to Dry River."

The dust cloud was beginning to diminish. Revulsion creased Murphy's face as he could once again view the world around him. "Skeet thought he was a smart man. Hell, he was 'bout as smart as Laszlo. Jones was gonna make money by marrying the Songbird of the West. Fat chance! Andrea and me knew how to make a dollar off that gal. Kidnap her. We put ever cent we had and then some into making that kidnapping work. But you ruined it, Dehner. Now, Andrea is dead. Ever thing is dead."

Murphy's voice didn't convey threat, it held something even darker. Rance spoke in a low, firm manner. "Drop the gun, Felix. We'll get you to a doctor—"

A loud explosive cry came from Murphy. "Oh sure, oh sure, get me to the doc! Patch me up so I can stand trial. The whole town can find out what a villain I am. It will be great for business! There will be reporters coming in from all over for the trial. Let's hang the snake who tried to kidnap the Songbird of the West! Well, that's not gonna happen!"

Felix Murphy began to raise his gun. Dehner understood. "No Murphy, no!"

For the last time, Felix Murphy gave the four-shot laugh as if mocking the detective. He then placed the gun barrel in his mouth and fired.

Chapter Twenty-Five

Carrie Whiting postponed her performance for that night. But she promised the residents of Dry River a free matinee the next day. Like her first appearance, the show would be open to families.

The show took place at mid-morning in the Silver Crown. The saloon was once again set up like a theater. And once again, the Silver Crown was packed out. Glenn Wilson, the town's newspaper man, was excited to the point of being irrational. He kept badgering Rance to help him get an interview with the Songbird of the West.

"You don't understand!" Wilson shouted at Dehner as they stood in the Silver Crown waiting for the show to begin. "I've been sending out stories about what's been going on here to newspapers all over. They'll want to know everything—"

"Miss Whiting appreciates your interest," as Dehner spoke he realized he sounded more like George McLeod than himself. "But she plans to say everything she needs to say during her performance."

Wilson threw up his arms in exasperation over Rance's ignorance. "You don't understand!" He repeated. "An interview now could boost my career, help me get a job with the *Dallas Herald* or the *Rocky Mountain News*."

Carrie entered the saloon through the side door beside the bar. She was accompanied by her agent, Tal Streeter, Ezra Brown and two of Brown's ranch hands.

Dehner spoke above the shouts and applause that now whirled around the saloon. "Mr. Wilson, I suggest you boost your career by doing your job."

Rance turned away and took his place in the last chair in the front row. He was sitting next to George McLeod. The detective quickly glanced at Carrie who was not glancing back. Dehner didn't take it personally. He knew the singer was at this moment focused entirely on her performance.

Ezra Brown jumped onto the small platform. He didn't have to gesture for quiet. His presence did that.

"Most of yus folks know who I am," the rancher began, "And most of yus know what's happened in this town. I jus' have a few things to say, then we can git to the purpose we came here for."

There was a small wave of polite laughter, after which Ezra continued. "On the request of Sheriff Tal Streeter I has agreed to be the acting mayor of Dry River. Don't nobody git all upset. We'll have us an election next month.

"A couple of my hands tole me they'd like to try being lawmen. When he gits him the time, Tal will talk with both of 'em and decide which one to give a deputy's badge to. The other one will be stuck with me."

A second wave of polite chortles quickly ended. "Now, to why we're all here. No fancy introductions are needed. Like the rest of yus, I'm sure looking forward to listening to Miss Carrie Whiting."

Loud applause sounded in the Silver Crown. Ezra Brown held Carrie's hand as she stepped onto the stage. Brown then gave a slight bow and began to place two fingers on his hat, only to realize that he wasn't wearing it. The acting mayor hastily retreated to his chair in the front row where he picked up his hat, then placed it on his lap as he sat down. He shot angry glances at the two ranch hands who had escorted Carrie. The hands wiped the smirks off of their faces. After all, one of them would still be working for Ezra.

Carrie opened by thanking the mayor and the people in attendance. She then paused briefly before continuing. "Before we begin, I would like to thank a man who yesterday saved my life and suffered a serious injury because of it. He is a man who will always have a special place in my heart. Laszlo, please stand up and allow me and your fellow citizens to express our appreciation!"

Laszlo, who was seated in the front row, got up to loud applause which Carrie led from the stage. The swamper gently patted his right arm, which was bandaged and in a sling, as if he were showing off a medal.

As Laszlo sat down, Carrie Whiting threw him a kiss. From the expression on the swamper's face, Dehner realized Laszlo would cherish the memory of Carrie Whiting's visit to Dry River for the rest of his life.

Most of Carrie's songs were happy and upbeat, which the citizens of the town very much needed. She sprinkled in a few lost-love songs for variety but saved the biggest change of pace for last.

"Loss is something we must all experience in our lives; I don't have to tell that to the people of Dry River," the singer spoke to her audience in a soft voice. "I was twelve when I experienced the loss of my parents. But, through a miraculous string of events, I was saved from a terrible life and placed in the home of Reverend Craig Barton and his wife Emma. They taught me the power of love. I'd like to express that love now in a song."

Carrie delivered a powerful rendition of *Amazing Grace* which she concluded by whispering, "Amen." For a moment the room was completely still, then loud applause erupted and many in the room enthusiastically returned the "Amen."

The singer stepped off the platform and began to talk with the people of Dry River. The crowd was polite and respectful. Even the men who had whistled and shouted out suggestive remarks at Carrie's previous performances were gentlemanly in their demeanor.

Ezra Brown smiled and shook his head as he watched the proceedings and spoke to Rance. "I've been the full owner of the Silver Crown for less 'n' two days and that gal's already causing me trouble."

"What do you mean?" Dehner asked.

"Carrie Whiting is turning my saloon into a church."

Dehner laughed along with the saloon's new full owner. Ezra Brown had a point.

Rance nervously paced about his hotel room. He could hear Carrie Whiting in the room next door singing as she packed her trunk. Her final concert in Dry River had been held in the morning in order for her to catch a stage which departed at one PM.

Earlier in the morning Carrie had asked the detective to help her carry her trunk down to the lobby after the concert. She hadn't explained why George McLeod couldn't help her but added, "There are a few things I'd like to talk with you about."

But she didn't say exactly when she wanted to

have this talk. Dehner stared at the saddle bags on his bed. He had already packed and repacked them twice.

Rance had turned down Tal Streeter's offer of being one of the men who escorted Carrie Whiting from her hotel to the Silver Crown. He thought it wise to keep his distance from the singer. Yet, he wanted very much to be close to her and anxiously looked forward to their talk. A whirlwind of contradictory emotions ran through Dehner and he was having trouble controlling them.

"Damn," the detective whispered to the floor.

From the next room, Rance could hear something heavy dragging on the floor and the door opening. Trying to look casual, the detective left his own room, saddle bags slung over his shoulder, and smiled at Carrie who was standing in the hallway beside a trunk.

"As promised, I am at your service," Dehner spoke in a light voice.

"You've already done so much for me. I never gave a thought to that odd laugh of Murphy's until you pegged him as Bob Hoover."

Dehner took a few steps toward the young woman and patted the object which now stood between them. "I guess this trunk is going to be put to a lot of use, what with your trip to New York coming up."

"Yes. That's what I want to talk with you

about. You see, this New York trip has me a bit nervous."

"Nothing to be nervous about, I'm sure the audiences in New York will love you just like they have everywhere else." The detective's use of the word "love" made him feel even more uneasy.

Carrie seemed to pick up on the uneasiness. She nervously caressed the trunk before speaking again. "Well . . . it goes beyond that. You see, the New York trip is a bit of an audition. George and I will be talking with some producers while we are there. I may be given the starring role in a new musical they are planning."

"There's still nothing to be nervous about, I'm sure you'll get the part."

The singer looked directly at Dehner and her voice took on a strong force. "That's what I'm nervous about! If I get the part, it means I'll have to leave Dallas and move to New York!" She stopped speaking and looked down as if embarrassed by the passion in her speech. "I'm just not sure if the Songbird of the West will be happy living in New York. Except for George, there will be no one there that I am close to."

Rance Dehner felt like Carrie Whiting had just presented him with an open door. An opportunity to become important to her, maybe even . . .

But the door seemed to stand only partially open and what could he possibly offer to a woman who already had money, fame and was in a position to get a lot more of both? "I'm sure you'll make the right decision, Carrie."

Something quickly ran over Carrie Whiting's face. Was it hurt, disappointment or . . . Dehner wondered if the singer herself knew. Whatever it was, it didn't stay there long. A beautiful if slightly artificial smile beamed at the detective. "Thank you, Rance. And be assured I will be looking for your name in the papers. I suspect your exploits even make the New York newspapers."

"You'll have to be reading the back pages."

Weak as the joke was, both of them laughed hard at it as Rance lifted the trunk and carried it downstairs, following behind Carrie. In the hotel lobby a large number of people were present to say goodbye to the Songbird of the West. Dehner learned that the two men Tal Streeter had appointed as deputies would be riding with Carrie and George McLeod to Dallas as guards against another kidnapping attempt.

As she left the hotel and began the short walk to the stage depot, Dehner realized he would not get a chance to say goodbye to the singer. George McLeod was now carrying the trunk and a throng of people surrounded Carrie Whiting. As he strolled behind the group, Rance could hear Carrie giving each one of her fans an exuberant reply to their attempts at conversation. It seemed foolish to barge into the circle and, like the others, demand the woman's time.

Glenn Wilson was waiting when the entourage arrived at the depot. Dehner remained back several paces, grimacing as Carrie quickly but politely stood by the doors of the stagecoach and answered a few of the newspaper man's questions.

"That's enough questions for now," George McLeod spoke with forced cordiality as he pointed upwards to the stagecoach driver and the shotgun, both of whom were ready to leave. "These gentlemen have a schedule to keep." He opened the door of the stagecoach for Carrie.

As she stepped up, Carrie Whiting looked over the heads of her flock of followers and glanced directly at Rance, as if she had known he was standing there. She gave the detective a playful smile and a wink, then she bent over and entered the coach. George McLeod got in beside her followed by the two deputies. Any further view Dehner might have of the singer was blocked.

Later that night, sitting by a campfire and drinking his second cup of coffee, Dehner thought back on the strange conversation with Carrie Whiting in the hallway outside of her hotel room and the farewell she had given him from the stagecoach. He tried to put it out of his mind or, at least, put it into perspective. The singer tried to be attentive and gracious to everyone. The smile and the wink was a nice gesture which she had, no doubt, forgotten by now.

But the detective knew he would never forget Carrie Whiting. He would replay their conversation in the hallway many times over in his mind, wondering what he should have said. And that playful smile and the accompanying wink would come back to him during the many lonely hours spent trying to sleep under a vast, dark sky.